The F
& The Flood

Hope you
enjoy!

Mil ♡

♡

Also by Miles Nelson

Riftmaster

The Forge
& The Flood

Miles Nelson

Elsewhen Press

The Forge & The Flood

First published in Great Britain by Elsewhen Press, 2022
An imprint of Alnpete Limited

Elsewhen Press, PO Box 757, Dartford, Kent DA2 7TQ
www.elsewhen.press

British Library Cataloguing in Publication Data.
A catalogue record for this book is available from the British Library.

ISBN 978-1-915304-00-1 Print edition
ISBN 978-1-915304-10-0 eBook edition

Designed and formatted by Elsewhen Press

Contents

To Chris,
May our love always burn bright,
as fluid and free as water.

Chapter 1

The Islands

The island of Veramilia was green once, a far cry from the cold grey rock that remained today.

Legends said that its inhabitants, the Ailura, had arrived ten generations ago. Driven from their old home by monsters and traitors who wanted to put an end to the Tribe's ancient traditions, the Ailura had set out in search of new soil, and found this island paradise of peace and plenty.

Over the years, their numbers boomed, their crops flourished, and they perfected techniques allowing them to build architectural marvels and multifunctional tools beyond their ancestors' wildest dreams. Their skill in forging defied all expectations of what could be accomplished with hardworking paws.

But they say the fire in the island slowly died.

The places that had once been green had long since collapsed into the ocean, leaving behind sheer cliffs and one secluded bay, nestled in the bosom of the great, jagged mountain. The island's collapse had left behind a single thriving village, its numbers dwindling as the generations passed.

The Ailura were a hardy race, but even they had limits.

With the loss of formerly plentiful resources, the techniques they had honed in their prime were gradually forgotten, along with the reason they settled on the island in the first place.

As he caught his breath, Sienna recalled his grandparents' stories, passed down from *their* great-grandfather, of seeing the last trees fall. By now, they were such a distant memory that he didn't know if he believed them, even when the ruins of that once-great civilization still stood proudly to this very day.

All Sienna and his surviving kin had known was cold grey stone, and the daily struggle to survive.

Watching the dawn light seeping over the distant ocean waves like molten copper, Sienna let out a weary sigh, knowing that the brief moment of respite was not enough. He'd been working since late last night, after a landslide sent mud and boulders crashing onto their already struggling fields.

The landslide had followed closely in the wake of an earthquake, an ever more frequent scourge on the island of Veramilia.

It was exhausting but necessary work. Without food, the village would not even survive the summer. Together they cleared rocks and mud, salvaged what could be salvaged and buried what could not.

Now, all these hours later, Sienna's fluffy sides heaved, black-furred paws dragging at the ground. The cream-coloured patches on his face and ears were caked with dust. He let his lever-stick, a copper pole used to shift boulders and create ruts for seeds, droop in his maw.

His orange-barred tail swished, flicking a puff of dust from his striped rump.

His amber eyes squinted against the brightness of the sunrise as he looked out over the horizon.

He had uttered few words of complaint over the hours, pausing only now, and only for a minute, to watch the sunrise. The Mothering Moon – the largest of three celestial bodies – had already disappeared below the horizon, but her smaller cub-moon still shone in tones of ivory, never setting except in the coldest winter nights.

Although he would never have voiced it, Sienna wanted desperately to swim off into that sunset, and leave this barren rock behind.

He couldn't, though.

None of them could.

Gradually, Sienna's gaze trailed down the mountainside towards the village.

Although not early risers by nature, troubled times lead to troubled minds, and the Ailuras' sleep schedule paid the price.

Sienna could already see them moving from where they worked, further up the rocky slopes.

Rivers of soft, furry bodies moved along winding paths between carefully-constructed mounds of stone, sprawling across the gently sloping mountainside. In tones of red, orange and gold, their fiery coats stood out from the grey of the mountain's slopes as they went about their business, striped tails waving like banners of fire. In times like this, the Ailura couldn't stop for a moment.

There weren't many of them; the tribe's numbers had dwindled in recent generations. But, the Ailura were stubborn, if nothing else.

"Sienna, focus," came an exhausted growl.

Sienna's pointed ears pricked, flicking off a wisp of dust. He turned, looking over his shoulder as an old Ailura limped up to stand by Sienna's left side. Sight adjusting to the early morning sunlight, Sienna narrowed his eyes and blinked until she came into focus.

"Yes, Mother."

His mother's face was gaunt with age, movements stiff, but still certain. Her short, creamy muzzle was beginning to turn grey. Her pelt, once gold, had faded over time to become a washed-out beige. Her underbelly and limbs were the tone of rich cocoa. Her tail wasn't as full as it had been when he was young, but was still fluffy, with exactly sixteen perfect bands of ivory.

She was stocky, and low-set, with thick and once-powerful forelimbs, although Sienna wondered just how much weight she had lost beneath her fur in recent months.

The Tribe had called his mother many things over the years... but her name perhaps spoke the loudest of them all.

"We need to get this done," Caldera said, with a huff.

"Yes. I'm just...–"

"–Tired. I know. We all are."

Sienna's ears drooped slightly. He knew that his mother's bones ached as well, from a lifetime of farm work. But the island was a cruel place; there was nothing they could do but plod on, setting the stage for the next day. Then the next week. Then the next generation.

It had been this way from time immemorial.

And soon it would be Sienna's turn to carry the mantle, whether he wanted to or not.

Sienna was brought back to the moment as Caldera turned away from him, flicking his nose with the tip of her tail as she went. Through crushed stems and piles of half-cleared debris she moved across the field of what-used-to-be-crops to the base of a stone almost as big as she was, which had obstructed a watering trench. She began to dig at the base of the stone, gesturing Sienna over with her tail as she made room for the copper pole he still held in his jaws.

Sienna's grasp on the object tightened, and he lumbered over to join her, wiggling the pole into the soil beneath the boulder until it was firmly stuck at a diagonal angle.

He raised his gaze to look at his mother, and their eyes met for a fleeting moment. They gave each other a nod of affirmation before both rose up onto their hindpaws and brought their combined weight down onto the metal stick.

The pole stayed upright for a few moments, as both creatures strained and heaved, striped tails lashing at the air. The pole creaked, a low and ominous sound. The boulder, though, shifted the slightest inch.

"Keep going! We've almost got it..." Caldera hissed, through gritted teeth.

Sienna grunted an acknowledgement, doubling down

on his weight. The boulder shifted an inch more. A trickle of water entered the hollow it had left behind.

And then... as they gave the metal pole one final push, there was a piercing crack. Sienna slumped face-first into the ground, Caldera crumpling into a fluffy heap beside him, and the boulder fell back into place on top of the protruding metal tool.

Caldera cursed under her breath, beginning to stagger up onto all four paws.

Sienna quickly followed, wincing as the impact stung in his soft black nose. After rubbing it for a moment, he nudged his nose against his mother's side to help her.

"By the Fire!" Caldera hissed.

The pole had split clean in two.

As soon as she was up, his mother began digging at the buried end of the pole. Some time later she staggered back, panting, and yanked the tool with her.

Sienna hesitated, shuffling his paws. He allowed her a moment, waiting until she'd finished muttering softly before warily speaking up. "...What shall we do?"

"What *can* we do? We can't grow crops if the water can't get to them!"

Sienna didn't think it would be the right moment to remind her that the stream hadn't been flowing properly in weeks. "We'll need another lever-stick, then," he said instead. "Perhaps you should take a walk down to the Blacksmith. It would be a nice break from the strain."

"And leave you to daydream? Bah. I'd be better off leaving the crops to the Nibblets."

Sienna sighed quietly to himself, ears lowering as he patiently waited for his mother's command. It wasn't the first time she'd made such a comment, nor would it be the last.

Caldera nudged the two halves of the tool over to Sienna a moment later with a forepaw. "You can take them. I have too much to do."

Sienna's ears lifted, a tingle of excitement running along his spine. He nodded. "Alright then."

He supposed it was also a chance to walk off the

cramps, and shake the dust from his fur.

"I won't be long," he assured Caldera, before stooping to gather the broken halves into his jaws.

Caldera let out a small snort. "I'll believe that when it happens," she teased, flicking him in the face with her tail as she moved off to clear a few of the smaller, more manageable stones. She did this by nudging them off the edge to send them tumbling down the mountainside. "...But I hope you keep your word this time."

Sienna, heat growing under his fur, grinned sheepishly back at her. Still, he didn't miss the soft warning in her tone.

"Yes, mother," he mumbled around the metal. "Burn Bright."

When Caldera didn't answer, Sienna turned his back on her. Placing his paws cautiously, he descended the zigzagging path into the village.

Many miles away, beyond the horizon Sienna had dreamed of reaching for so long, a creature of a far different breed played among the waves.

The early morning sun was just beginning to light up the sea, sending bluish pillars of brightness filtering down into the darkness below.

The light was caught, captured, stretched into wavering strands by fronds of red kelp that swayed gently in the current, their stems dropping off into the abyss far below.

Indigo floated, pausing where he swam to bask in the light dappling across his hide. It was beautiful here; he almost didn't want to leave. Outstretched paws, rubbery and webbed, gently sculled at the water, keeping his long body afloat. Small, round ears were closed up against his head, preventing the ocean water getting in, but he could still hear – no, feel – the force of the waves breaking and crashing above him.

When he looked up, he could see webs of seafoam forming on the water's surface. He felt the ebb and rise of the tide in his whiskers.

Lights glimmered and flashed at the very edges of his vision as small, shimmering creatures formed into shoals that rippled and pulsed. Thousands of tiny lights blinked as their formation swelled, forming a hypnotic and ever-shifting spectre in an effort to confuse the predator in their midst.

Indigo's deep blue eyes followed them for a moment. His nose wrinkled, drawing in water, while his gills flared at the sides of his serpentine neck.

A moment later, he began to swim with a powerful kick of his webbed hind feet, his tapering tail steering him down, away from the sunlight and the glowing shoals of fish. As much as he would have loved to stay and snack, he was here for a reason and he wasn't about to go home with empty paws.

Indigo wasn't usually one to keep promises, but tonight was an exception. It was the night of the Festival.

And like any self-respecting Lutra, Indigo couldn't pass up the opportunity to celebrate, not for anything. Not even a sight as lovely as this.

With lithe, undulating motions he swam into the shadow of the kelp. His hide darkened, and his true colours were revealed. His body was a dark steel blue, perfectly suited for a life in the waves. It lightened to a paler shade below, his underbelly a faded baby blue. Speckles of the same tone scattered his back and neck, with a few larger blots on the rump.

As one of his fathers had declared so proudly, he was like a midnight snowstorm.

As he descended, Indigo felt the gloom closing in, and soon the seafloor was rising up to meet him. Here he paused once more, fanning out his webbed paws to bring himself to a halt as he scanned the murky sediment. Twisting around, he peered into the shadows, but nothing stood out to him.

No telltale lights winking in the dark.

A moment later, he paddled on, glancing around warily.

He knew that strange and dangerous creatures could be found in the deep ocean.

He wove around the towering stems of the kelp, investigated the places where their roots disappeared into the sand. When he found a rock, he would paw at it, lifting it up from the seabed and examining it before dropping it with a small explosion of debris. Then he swam on.

After some time, he found a rock light enough to carry, and took it with him, tossing it from paw to paw for a time and rolling over onto his back.

When he tired of this game, he simply carried it.

He caught sight of a sickly-white carapace on the seafloor, and a flash of an insectoid leg. A creature almost twice his size disappeared under the sand, throwing up clouds of sediment before he could catch a good glimpse of it.

He steered well clear, searching until he finally came upon a red shell, quite small, but wonderfully spiralling. Enthused, Indigo picked it up, and held it up to his nose for a closer look. Not a moment later he felt a small stinging sensation in his paw. Seemed that shell had already been taken. Turning the shell over, he saw the small jaws of a baby sea-worm dangling from his pad; the shell hid the rest of its plump red body. Startled, Indigo let a stream of bubbles escape his nostrils. Sea-worms could be tasty, but they were not what Indigo was here for today. After working its jaws free, Indigo let the shell float to the seabed and watched it burrow back under the sand, moving on despite the sudden droop in his limbs.

He carried on, lithe motions weaving him freely around the stems of the kelp.

Some time later, Indigo came upon something different. In a clearing where some light managed to reach the seabed, he found clusters upon clusters of shells! All of them adorned with colourful patterns, and all of them wonderfully unique. Purple-blue tendrils curled out of each shell and swayed in the current, seeking falling scraps from the upper ocean. With a shiver of excitement, Indigo surged forward. Those that felt his wake hastily closed up or retreated back into the sand by frantically whipping their tendrils, but some of them weren't quite quick enough.

Indigo managed to seize one in his paws, and with a kick of his hindpaws, surged up towards the surface. The sea grew brighter around him as, kick by kick, pulse by pulse, he ascended.

He broke the surface in an arcing leap of joy, sending crystalline droplets cascading into the waves, scattering rainbows in the morning sun. His gills emptied themselves of water; instead he gulped at the air, whiskers combing the chilly morning breeze. His neck and back shed water easily, becoming velvety and dry within moments.

As his lungs adjusted to the air, Indigo took in the sight of his homeland, its vast form sprawling in the waves mere miles away. The lush island of Indigna was beautiful from here. Its mountain peak was soft where it scraped the sky, a blanket of rainforest shrouded in a thick fog that hid the unbelievable array of colours to be found within.

After a moment, he turned his attention back towards his prize.

In a swift movement he rolled over onto his back, bringing the shellfish and rock onto his chest. With nimble paws he shattered the shell, peeling back tentacles and purple-blue flesh.

He let the scraps and beautiful shell-shards go, dropping them back into the water to feed its kin.

This creature's meat was toxic to the Lutra; its bright colours were a warning. But he didn't want to eat it. Indigo thought for a moment that this one was a dud; that it didn't have what he was looking for.

At least half of its shell can be salvaged, Indigo thought, whiskers twitching with irritation.

But then he caught a gleam of light beneath the mess.

The Lutra's heart raced. He sent the last scraps

splashing down into the sea, and finally found what he was looking for: a pearl, shimmering with iridescence. Holding it delicately with rubbery paws, he tilted it towards the sun, watching the colours change and gleam. It was as though a rainbow had been captured inside the tiny orb.

With renewed enthusiasm, Indigo washed off his prize in the sea, hid it in his cheek so that he wouldn't lose it, and dived back underwater, swimming straight down into the swaying kelp forest until the fronds rose up around him.

Soon he could see the seabed once again, and the flashes of colour which belonged to cautiously re-emerging shellfish.

Indigo hung above them, keeping his distance for a moment.

He watched, waited.

One by one, they reappeared, shedding streams of sand.

Indigo selected his target, the largest of the group, and prepared himself to lunge. He was dimly aware of a twinkling in the cover of the kelp as something moved there, but Indigo did not react.

I'll be out of here soon. One more, one moment... just one... –

Indigo lurched forward. The shellfish once again began to flee back beneath the sand... but not from him. A dark shape surged forward out of the kelp, spinning sand from the ocean floor with an enormous sweep of its tailfin. Indigo seized the brightly-patterned shell in his forepaws and, through instinct alone, managed to twist his body out of the way of a deadly sharp snout and wide, armoured head.

Terrifying jaws full of jagged teeth snapped shut onto empty space where Indigo's tail had been a moment earlier.

Indigo twisted to a halt, almost swallowing his prized pearl in the process and glanced back, and immediately wished he hadn't.

This creature – this *monster* – was what his kind called

a winking spearfish... far too innocent a name, in Indigo's opinion, for a creature so terrifying. A speckling of shimmering scales down its sides winked in the pale sunlight as it moved, one of the reasons the Lutra had given the winking spearfish its name. These served as bait for smaller and stupider prey than Indigo. The other reason was the deadly point on the end of its snout.

This spearfish, much to his distaste, was a particularly large one.

The creature circled back, turning gradually towards him. Luckily though, the armoured cartilage running down its head and back limited its mobility. The larger the spearfish, the harder it found it to turn. And this one, fortunately (or, perhaps, unfortunately?) was enormous.

But the Spearfish could never outmanoeuvre a Lutra so long as they were prepared.

That meant he had no time to lose. In an instant he was kicking his hindpaws and shooting through the kelp forest, twisting around massive leaves and through tightly-clustered stems. His whiskers guided him, tail steering him through the tightest of gaps and even tighter turns, while his gills worked frantically.

Indigo could hear thudding and hissing behind him as the spearfish gave chase, close on his tail, but quite unable to replicate the Lutra's tight turns. But while Indigo had to veer frantically, the Spearfish was capable of simply ploughing through everything in its path. It was gaining on him fast.

Indigo's heart hammered.

Suddenly, the shell clutched close to his chest didn't seem quite worth the effort, nor did the pearl digging into his cheek.

The hollow rushing sound of the blood in his ears drowned out any other sound, but for a moment he thought he felt the stems parting around him as it closed in.

He squeezed in between two kelp stems, and found the foliage growing thicker. Their branches hung heavy with crimson seed pods that filled every available space. Soon not even he could find a place to fit through to the other side.

Indigo was cornered.

Panic drowned out everything else.

A dull crash echoed from somewhere in the kelp forest. It was close.

Sick with fear, the Lutra twisted his lithe body, and turned back on himself. As the spearfish's jaws loomed out of the dark, its sharpened snout cleaving a stem of kelp clean in two, Indigo surged towards it.

He felt the rush of water as its spear missed him by a hair's breadth... then he was up and over, undulating past it, and out of the kelp forest.

By the time it had broken through the barrier and doubled back on its path, Indigo was already long gone.

The village of Ailuria wasn't much to look at. At a glance, it was nothing more than a maze of domes built into the earth, winding paths weaving between them. These stone houses had served their village for generations, but the techniques that made them were, like so much else, lost to the ages.

The village wasn't a pretty place, but it was functional and sturdy.

Sienna couldn't help feeling the faint, foreboding inkling that the buildings would even outlast the Ailura themselves.

Their numbers had been shrinking for a long time; many of these homes now stood empty or collapsed, with only rock-sliders living there now.

As Sienna pressed further into the village, he spotted the creatures' silky, dappled grey bodies coiled over every available surface. Both horizontally and vertically, rock-sliders' ridged underbellies clung to the stone in the best positions to soak up the early morning sunlight.

They were toxic, unfortunately, or the Ailura might have been a bit more well-fed. Instead they lived in uneasy peace with the serpentine invaders.

Where no Ailura lived any more, rock-sliders thrived.

As he moved past the more rural parts of town, Sienna couldn't help but feel their dark eyes following him, shining like wet river pebbles.

At least, Sienna mused, the rock-sliders didn't eat their crops. The soil alone was generally rich enough in nutrients for them, although it was with unnerving frequency that Sienna found them gnawing on bones.

To Sienna's quiet relief, he saw fewer of them as he pressed further into the more populated parts of Ailuria.

He made his way towards a series of tall, soot-stained pillars of stone which belched smoke into the cloudless sky.

Fire had many uses; as well as forging, it could tan leather and preserve meat when it was caught. It could bend inedible twigs and sticks into crafting materials, and harden them to be used as weapons and tools. It could purify seawater in times of drought, and smelt ores into metals when they were found. The ash itself was useful for crops, and the stench kept away any predators that roamed the slopes.

Fire was the reason that his kind had survived for so long.

Other Ailura brushed against Sienna as he wound his way along the narrow paths between the small, domed homes. Tired faces gazed out at him from within rounded entryways, and others shouldered past him as they carried various objects and materials in mouths or woven saddlebags, disappearing with a whisk of a striped tail.

He passed a slate-grey Ailura digging frantically in a pile of rubble. By his burnt paws, Sienna could tell that he was a blacksmith, but struggled to see what he was actually doing. Sienna didn't need to wonder for long, though, as the stranger finally stepped back, dragging a pale infant from the ruins. A moment later, he bounded away, leaving the powerful scent of smoke in his wake.

Soon, Sienna found his way to one of the smoking

columns. Standing by the entrance, he took a moment to marvel. He craned his head back, as he had many times before. The building, a towering chimney of grey stone and clay, rose into the sky. It was many times his height, and Sienna couldn't imagine how the ancient Ailura could have possibly built such a thing.

Sienna looked down as an old Ailura emerged from the smoking tower and pushed briskly past. The stranger offered a small nod as the younger Ailura stepped aside. "Mmph... I'm too old for this," he mumbled around the bundle of metal fragments in his muzzle, with noticeable difficulty and a small wink.

And then he was gone, leaving Sienna wondering what had happened to his once-proud banner of a tail. A long-healed scar had left it half the length it should have been.

After checking to ensure the way ahead was clear, he finally pressed forward, squeezing into the narrow entryway. He followed a short pathway deeper inside, the tunnel walls hugging tightly around him, tickling his whiskers. Soon he could see the air trembling, and the stench of smoke hit him with comforting familiarity. The heat radiating from within warmed him to the core.

The entry tunnel soon opened up into an almost cavern-like room, oval-shaped and several times Sienna's length from nose to tail. It took a moment for Sienna to pick out the blacksmith's shape from the dark and flickering shadows cast by the fire at the back of the room.

It was a spray of sparks that gave her away, though, along with the sound of stone scraping against metal. She was settled in a shadowed spot away from the fire, with her forepaws resting against a plate of iron set on top of a large, flat stone. When she raised a paw, she revealed a stone tied to her paw pad with woven plant fibres. She was using this makeshift whetstone to flatten and sharpen the still-glowing metal, sending sparks flying over her dark mahogany fur.

Sienna lowered his head, dropping the broken tool onto the stony ground.

The Blacksmith's dark brown ears pricked as the clatter

echoed throughout the forge. Her expression was hidden by flickering shadows in the firelight, but Sienna knew her well enough to imagine an expression of irritation at being interrupted in her task.

"Blaze?" Sienna called, announcing his presence.

Crimson eyes flashed in the firelight.

"Sienna! Is that you?" Sienna heard confusion, then excitement.

Blaze's dark shape settled back onto her haunches, and she used her teeth to pull the whetstone from where it was tied to her paw. She placed it on the stone slab by her current project, and bounded over to greet Sienna.

The two touched noses, and Sienna drew in her smoky scent. He had known that smell, loved it even, since they were both fresh out of the nest. They had been best friends once, but now, Sienna liked to think of her as more than that. Besides Caldera, Blaze was the closest thing to family he had.

"I didn't expect to be seeing you here today!" Blaze's eyes narrowed slightly in the dark. "What's broken this time?"

Sienna chuckled guiltily. "My mother's lever-stick."

"Oh, good. I thought it was going to be something complex."

Sienna chuckled again and shook his head as he nudged the two halves towards Blaze with the end of his nose.

As his friend picked up the metal pieces and bustled over to the fire, Sienna turned his attention to the smears of soot on the walls. It was an odd habit of Blaze's to leave them in her forge. The walls were covered in markings hard to make out in this light. Most were small, simple diagrams, and scribbles, although Sienna could only guess at what the rest meant.

Notes and blueprints, perhaps?

"So, how's Caldera?" Blaze asked as she waited for the metal to soften.

"As grumpy, foul tempered and stubborn as ever."

Blaze giggled. "I'd be worried if she was acting any other way."

Sienna smiled in turn, watching her work with fascination. As the last in a long line of farmers, Sienna had been his mother's apprentice ever since he could remember. Smithing, though, was another matter entirely.

As was tradition, Blaze had inherited her parents' forge when she herself was very young. Although Caldera had raised her alongside Sienna, allowing her to help with the crops, she was always destined to become a blacksmith. Fortunately though, unlike her adoptive brother, she was truly in her element in the forge.

As she gazed into the fire, Sienna watched her truly come alive.

After arranging the two halves of his mother's tool in a small stone pot, Blaze retrieved a thin metal stick, held it firmly in her jaws, and began to poke at the two halves of broken metal. She didn't even flinch as the burning wood spat; the embers settled peacefully onto her fireproof fur and burned out.

Holding her own tool in her jaws and never quite letting it rest long enough to melt itself, Blaze's focus was entirely on her work.

Blaze was in a league of her own when it came to blacksmithing; Sienna was certain that not even the ancients who first settled here would be as proficient at their craft.

She had always had big dreams, but her biggest had been started and re-started more times than Sienna could count. Still he always asked the same question.

"How's the side project going, then?"

Blaze froze, as though she'd been stung. And as always, she gave the same answer.

"I... ah. Well, you know. I decided to try something new." She spoke cautiously, mumbling around the metal rod in her jaws. "It's nothing, really. Probably won't work."

"Oh, yeah?"

Blaze was silent, carried on poking at the flames until Caldera's lever-stick glowed orange with the heat. It soon melted into a glowing pool.

All that time, she said nothing, silence punctuated only by the crackling of the forge.

Sienna gave her a gentle nudge with his shoulder, and broke the quiet. "Hey, if anyone can pull it off, it's you."

"You say that, but..."

Blaze paused, using her rod to deftly ease the bowl of molten metal out of the flames and onto a stone platform. "Help me with this," she muttered.

Sienna obliged. By nudging the platform with noses and paws, she and Sienna manoeuvred the molten metal away from the fire and then, tilting the platform upright, poured it into a mould composed of greyish clay. The molten metal hissed, and a hairline fracture splintered one edge of the mould... but other than that, the stone held its shape.

When he was sure that the lever-stick would cool nicely, Sienna looked up at Blaze. "You know," he began carefully. "I wouldn't ask about this if I wasn't certain you'd manage it one day."

"I... I suppose..." Blaze finally admitted.

"So...?"

She raised her ears, the ghost of a smile playing across her lips. Her eyes gleamed crimson in the firelight. "Well... I do have... just a little bit of a good feeling about this one. But if it fails..."

"...If it fails, you can try again. There's no need to rush. The Ailura have lived here for generations. We'll be alright for a few years yet."

"...Perhaps. It's just..."

Blaze paused, hesitating.

"...aren't you getting a bad feeling about these quakes, Sienna?"

"...Well... yes, but... the legends say we've–"

"The quakes aren't in the legends, Sienna."

Sienna thought back to everything that Caldera had taught him over the years. Of all the things he knew of the trials and tribulations of their history, and the struggles of their ancestors, earthquakes were never mentioned.

"I... don't know, Blaze. But I'm sure they'll pass."

"Perhaps."

Blaze trailed off, but didn't seem satisfied. Her reaction left Sienna with a sinking feeling in his gut despite his own words.

After that, she fell silent for a time as they waited for the lever-stick to cool.

Soon it was time. Nothing more to do other than break the mould. Blaze began to do so, tying a wide, flat stone firmly to her paw and pulling it tight with her teeth. When it was held firmly in place no matter how hard she shook it, Blaze finally spoke.

"I just... I can't stand this place. The sooner we can get off this island, the better."

Sienna looked at her, creamy ears folding back. He nudged at the side of her head with the tip of his pale snout.

"I know," he said quietly. "Same here."

Blaze's ears went back as well, but she didn't say anything more. She took a deep breath of smoke-incensed air and then brought the stone down, sending sparks spraying in all directions.

It was only when the kelp forest was left far behind and Indigo had reached the shallows around Indigna, that he finally felt safe enough to slow down. Spearfish rarely ventured close to shore.

He barely took heed of the colourful corals and bright shoals of flashing flitfish as he coasted the last crests of the waves breaking in the shallows. The ocean floor loomed close enough that pink corals tickled at his belly, momentarily startling him. And then, finally, his blue-grey paws touched down into the sand.

Indigo finally staggered to shore beside the mouth of the Lutra's River. It was a little over an hour since he'd fled the kelp forest, and now his short limbs trembled with exhaustion. He expelled the water from his gills with a short huff, spitting out the pearl he had gathered and dropping the rainbow clam. Finally, he sank onto his belly in the soft white sand, whilst the ocean's gentle waves swelled around him.

A faint tropical breeze toyed with the treetops, hissing.

Creatures sang in a raucous chorus from the luscious undergrowth.

It was good to be home.

Remembering the initial aim of his excursion, Indigo rolled over onto his back to study the clam he had dragged ashore, shell clasped tightly shut. He inspected it. It was decorated extravagantly with patterns of yellow, purple and blue.

Realizing that he had nothing to open it with, the Lutra wandered further ashore until he came to a deposit of rounded pebbles, and after a moment of deliberation, selected one. He settled back on his haunches, and then brought the two together. The clam shell shattered, and he let out a breath.

Indigo sifted through the goop and limp tendrils that remained, picking it apart before he was finally certain that there was nothing inside to be had.

His head and tail drooped, whiskers lowering as he returned to the items he'd already collected. At least the pearl was pretty, and the shell... well... it was something.

There was too little time to go on another excursion, so he'd just have to make do.

Indigo gathered the objects back into his cheeks as he waded back into the water. This time he kept his head above the surface as he paddled against the current of the river and made his way inland. His eyes combed the riverbanks for the tree that marked the entrance to the village of the Lutra.

It wasn't far away.

Although the tree itself had died long ago, its branches had become a cradle for a living paradise. Fruit-bearing vines hung from its gnarled trunk, branches hanging heavy with trailing mosses and lichens. The tree leaned heavily over the river, its branches trailing in the water, for the riverbank had fallen away beneath it in the same storm that had killed it. This had left the exposed entrance of a subterranean cave shielded by thick, algae-covered roots.

Indigo had to push through a curtain of hanging vines and lichens trailing in the water. Doing so lightly disturbed them, and sent thousands of tiny, serpentine creatures fluttering skyward. Their golden bodies shone in the sunshine, thousands of wings letting out a melodic hum. Once he reached the cave, the Lutra ducked under the water, swimming in between its roots and making his way into the cave against the constant pull of the current.

Despite the sudden plunge into darkness, Indigo felt his whiskers tickling against the walls of a narrow tunnel, and it was almost second nature to follow its twists and turns. He felt a distant rumble trembling up through the water as he pressed on, a distant and comforting roar throbbing through his bones. Soon he scrambled up onto solid ground. The pool he'd just emerged from, as well as being connected to the main river, was fed by a tiny stream.

With its chill nipping at his toes, Indigo moved further up a gently sloping path until it opened out into a wide cavern.

Anyone trekking through the rainforest above could never have guessed a subterranean paradise existed below.

It was unknown, lost to history, whether these caverns were naturally formed or built by the Lutra themselves. But, it was common knowledge that the waterfall, pouring in from above, was of their making. Their storytellers said that the Lutra had dammed up a tributary of the river and created a water source for their family. And now, generations later, that waterfall gave life to the whole village.

Chubby pups played in the rapids which poured from the plunge pool at the village's heart, while the colourful, sinewy bodies of their parents worked at waterwheels further down. The foaming water surrounded the village with a protective moat, winding in a series of tiny falls between the Lutra's various homes. One final waterfall spanned the village in breadth and emptied into a pool below the path Indigo now walked, where it would soon rejoin the river. Here the weight of the water gradually powered contraptions of stone and vines, lifting woven carriers full of fruit and fish up to the main area of the village. Hunters and scavengers awaited at the top and bottom to pull their otherwise heavy loads onto dry land.

The village itself was laid out in levels, homes built upon numerous flat plateaus rising up towards the waterfall pool.

From some angles, the homes barely looked like homes at all; first constructed from river clay and mud, they had been carefully decorated with still-living flowers, shells, pearls, and lush feathers. Whilst they could take months to build and dry, the end result was both sturdy and malleable, especially when it came to decoration.

The families with more elaborately decorated homes tended to get more attention from their neighbours, and even occasional offerings of flowers or fish as a sign of respect. But no-one wanted to be the one who always stayed the same; fashions were ever-changing. This year's trend seemed to have a focus on flowers. Indigo didn't particularly care about home fashion, though; he was just quietly glad that skulls were no longer in style.

As he made his way up through the levels of the village, he passed a small family consisting of a mother and two pups working together to pat a mound of clay into shape. Whether they were making themselves a new home, or one for the young ones to inherit when the time came, Indigo did not know. He wasn't particularly concerned either way.

Indigo quickly passed them by, making his way up towards the waterfall.

He soon reached the plunge pool, and followed the path around it. Here, at the base of the waterfall, another mechanism had been built up against the rock face by ancient paws. Composed of a series of vines, weights, and slow-moving platforms, it gradually moved under the power of the waterfall. After a moment's hesitation, Indigo clambered onto a platform as it rose to meet him, and allowed it to carry him up the rocky wall. He stepped from the platform to a rocky ledge and entered a hidden tunnel. The entrance was slippery with algae and decorated with pearls and shells, the colour of which was worn away by time and water.

The sound of the rushing water faded as he left the waterfall behind and pressed into the hidden grotto.

Indigo finally stepped onto a carpet of soft green moss.

It was surprisingly dry here; Indigo's ancestors had gone to great lengths to ensure that their family line possessed not just a beautiful home, but a functional one. The walls had been arranged with shelves of mud and clay, and these were lined with a myriad of treasures collected over the years. Glowing pearls, neon-toned feathers, spiralling antlers, shards of rainbow coral and crystals picked up from the seashore; Indigo's fathers collected only the strangest and most beautiful things that could be found in the sea and on the island of Indigna.

At the back of the room, two rounded doorways stood half-hidden by curtains of flowering vines.

Indigo paused to drop his pearl and shell piece on the ground before him. As he straightened up, he called out.

"Dad, Pa! I'm back!" His voice was quickly lost to the mosses and the distant din of the waterfall.

For a while, there was only silence. Then, a soft murmur of voices rose from beyond the lichen curtain. Hushed words that he couldn't quite make out from here. Indigo waited until he grew worried, then inched nearer.

"...And... our son, he... you know..."

"Yes, I know."

"But I can't do it."

"...I understand, Tide... you know that."

As the voices trailed off into silence, Indigo got the distinct feeling that he wasn't supposed to be hearing this.

"Pa?"

He waddled forward, dipping his head as he prepared to enter.

Abruptly the lichens parted, and suddenly Indigo was nose to nose with another. Purple eyes blinked back at him as though dazed from a heavily whiskered, lilac face. Indigo moved backwards, giving his father room to enter their main living space. Similar to his son's pale dappling, a light speckling of deep blue dusted the older Lutra's back, especially around his rump.

A necklace of woven seaweed was bound tightly to his pale neck, pearls and crystals tinkling gently as he moved out into the open.

It was a half-joking rumour among the Lutra that Indigo's father had swallowed a pearl when he was newly-born, leaving him with an obsession with all that glittered. It was, at least, befitting of his name.

"Pa!"

"Indigo! You're back late! Are you hurt?" Shimmer asked. "Should I call for Shard?"

"What? No! Of course not!"

"Oh, okay. Good. I'm sorry, I was..."

Indigo noticed him glance back towards his sleeping chamber. "...busy. Preparing for the festival."

Indigo blinked. "...Dad?"

Shimmer slightly inclined his head.

Indigo lowered his voice. "Is he coming this year, then?"

His father paused. Slowly, he shook his head.

Indigo's heart sank. Every year, his other father did this. And every year, he promised to do better.

"Maybe you should just order him to go. You can do that, right? You're the Queen!"

The title of Queen was, for the most part, a ceremonial title; the Lutra had little need for true leadership any more. But, along with the annual task of appearing at the festival each year, Queen Shimmer had the luxury of being able to make minor decisions, and the somewhat limited ability to boss the other Lutra around.

"Well, yes, but..." his father's tail twitched. His brows

creased. "…That's not how it works."

"Why not? It's the Festival of Love, and he's your partner!"

"That's why I don't force him."

"But… If you don't go together, what's the point?"

"You'll understand one day, Indigo. Just trust me, for now. The festival wouldn't make him happy if I forced him to go. Now, what was it you wanted?"

"I, uh, just wanted to show you the last things I found for my festival chain."

Shimmer's expression brightened. "Oh?"

Indigo picked up his pearl and the shell in a rubbery paw and, settling back on his haunches, held it out to his father.

Shimmer leaned in close. Indigo watched his whiskers twitch in thought, his expression either thoughtful or awed.

"Oh… That's a beauty," Shimmer crooned. "Small, but the colours are bright. It'll make a great centrepiece."

Indigo basked in the praise, his whiskers lifting.

"Are you gonna show your dad?" Shimmer asked a moment later.

"Yeah, of course! If he wants to see it, that is."

As Shimmer's whiskers lowered, Indigo knew immediately that he'd said the wrong thing. A stone of guilt lodged itself in his belly. Before Shimmer could scold him, Indigo continued.

"…I mean… Wouldn't he rather wait until my chain is finished?"

"Oh… Perhaps. A surprise, you mean?"

His father paused, considering.

"Yes. Yes, that sounds like a grand idea! Tide would love that!"

Indigo nodded.

"I'd best get it finished, then."

"Yes, of course! Too much to do, so little time. I should get back to your father; he'll have my head if he can't get mine done," Shimmer said, with gentle humour, and a small glimmer in his eye. "See you later, alright?"

"Yes, yes! Of course!"

His father turned with the sleek elegance only a Queen could display, glittering decorations gently tinkling around him. He ducked his head and disappeared beyond the curtain of lichens.

A moment later, Indigo pushed through the other curtain and into his own sleeping area.

For the next few hours, Indigo worked alone, weaving together golden strands of dry seaweed with dextrous paws. He took all of the colourful things and glittering trophies he had collected over the months and set them into the festival chain. The pearl, he placed in the very centre of the woven chain, and around it he arranged shells, flowers, and attractive river pebbles. These, he tied in place, or stuck down with a mashed-up pulp of burberries and sea salt. When this sticky substance hardened, it would bind powerfully enough to last years.

Just as Indigo began to fear that his time would run out and that he would miss the festival entirely, it was done.

The final task was to put it on.

Dipping the end of the chain into a large half-shell filled with burberry pulp, Indigo pressed the ends together and waited impatiently for them to bind.

Whiskers quivering with excitement, Indigo raised the end of the chain as high as his forelegs would stretch, and then ducked his head under it. The first row of the chain, composed of seashells, fell into place against his chest. Indigo twisted the chain over itself, wrapping it around his neck once more. With a soft clacking sound, another line of colourful shells fell against the first. Another twist, another loop, and the third layer fell into place, this one of smaller shells, with the pearl resting beautifully in the centre.

After one final layer had been twisted and rearranged,

Indigo's festival attire was done.

The pearl sparkled in the light, resting neatly against his chest, the shells clacking gently as he moved.

His chain had formed a spiralling necklace of four layers in all; and although it wasn't as impressive as some, certainly not his father's, Indigo was pleased with it.

A moment later and he was ducking out of his room to find Shimmer already waiting for him. Although his stance was regal as he waited, his expression was positively bursting with excitement.

Indigo stared, with awe, at his festival garb.

Shimmer's chain was always something to behold, and this year was no different. He wore three chains in all; one decorated the Queen's chest with an arrangement of coral, and dangled with a few crystals trailing down over his forelegs. A chain wound in layers around his belly tinkled gently along his sides as he moved, his ribs and spine decorated with rows of pearls. And then one final chain, of golden seaweed and a scattering of seashells, started at the base of his tail and wound all the way to the tip.

A small, white flower had been inset with a tiny pearl, and placed atop his father's head.

"Wow," Indigo breathed. "I swear, your chains get crazier every year."

Shimmer chuckled. "Well, you can thank Tide for that!"

It was tradition among the Lutra that lovers made each others' chains for the yearly festival.

And Tide, despite not going to the festival itself, had perfected the art. His necklaces were beautiful, his arrangements unique and skilled, and his work a perfect representation of all the things that his partner loved.

Indigo wondered, wistfully, what sort of chain Shimmer would have made for Tide, given the chance.

"Well?" Shimmer asked, abruptly. "Are you ready?"

Jerked from his thoughts, Indigo nodded vigorously.

His father poked his head through the curtain of lichens.

"Tide? He's ready!"

Indigo stood to attention, trying to look as proud in his chain as Shimmer had.

His father gently pulled back the curtain, and a dark blue head peeked out. His ears were laid back, eyes blinking anxiously as though he was uncertain of where to look. As he caught sight of Indigo, though, his expression lit up.

"Oh, don't you look wonderful! What a beautiful chain!"

"He gets it from you," Shimmer said fondly, offering his partner an encouraging nod.

Tide left his sleeping chamber with small, shuffling steps.

Indigo was, at first, confused by his nervousness, until he had stepped out in his entirety.

Tide wasn't large, for a Lutra; in fact, he was quite small compared to his mate. He was thin, and almost bedraggled looking, with nothing in the way of markings or colours. Like a stormy night sky, he was a dark blue-grey colour with eyes that twinkled sky-blue like twin moons.

A woven chain of blue flowers and bright green leaves hung around his father's neck.

Tide shuffled his paws, smiling nervously at his son.

"What do you think?"

"Dad!" Indigo exclaimed. "What's this for?"

Tide let out a small chuckle. "Well, I... your father wanted to make me a chain, this year. He thought it might make me feel more involved. What do you think? Do you like it...?"

"I love it, dad! You look amazing," Indigo clamoured, hurrying forward to appreciatively nudge Tide's neck.

Tide's eyes widened with surprise, but he lowered his head to rest his chin atop his son's head in turn.

"Does that mean you're coming to the festival this year?" Indigo ventured, stepping back.

Indigo caught a look of fleeting nervousness cross his face. "Er... well..."

With a soft chiming sound, Shimmer moved over to

stand beside his partner, gently bumping their sides together. After a moment of hesitation, Tide wound his tail over Shimmer's.

"Maybe next year, eh?" Shimmer said gently.

Indigo tried to hide his disappointment, but his whiskers must have drooped, because Shimmer glanced sideways to Tide with an encouraging smile.

"Uh... maybe. We'll see," Tide said, hesitantly. "You two will just have to have enough fun for the three of us, hm?"

Indigo sighed, but nodded slightly.

"I'm sure we will, dad."

"Just... Tell me all about it when you get home, alright?"

"Don't we always?"

Tide's expression brightened, and he slightly inclined his head. He gradually unwound his tail from Shimmer's.

"You two should start heading out. You don't want to miss the festivities," Tide said.

Shimmer chuckled. "The festivities can't even start without me!" he said, playfully nudging at Tide's neck. "...But you're right."

Indigo's tail twitched with impatience as he waited for his fathers to finish their goodbyes.

"Bye, dad!" Indigo called.

Shimmer and Tide rubbed foreheads, and gently bumped noses. Then Shimmer moved away, leaving his mate to watch them go.

A moment later, Indigo scampered off down the tunnel, hearing Shimmer's gently chiming form following close behind. The tunnel opened up to reveal the waterfall, glistening, roaring and scattering rainbows. Soon, Indigo was lowered to the level of the main village by the waterfall mechanism, and he was bounding around the waterfall pool.

The light shining down from above the waterfall had changed; what was once a pristine pillar of white daylight now glistened red and gold. The sun was going down, and soon, it would be silvery moonlight.

When Indigo had returned from his venture, the village had been beautiful, yet quite bare; since he had gone inside to work on his chain, flowers had been brought in from the outside world and laid out around paths and doorways.

Already, Lutra were gathering on an open plateau beneath the waterfall, surrounded by foaming rapids. Pale and dark, large and small, bright and dull; from grey to teal to violet to indigo, they mingled in a myriad of cool colours.

Pups played with their siblings and friends while their parents talked, wrestled and played. Young lovers wound around one another in serpentine adoration.

As Indigo entered the throng, he felt voices ebbing away around him, conversations trailing off into silence until Shimmer's delicate chiming could be heard harmonizing with the song of the waterfall. Indigo caught a soft murmur flood over the crowd, and he knew immediately what they were saying.

Alone, again?

Youngsters ceased to play, and all eyes turned on Shimmer.

The Queen padded up to the front of the crowd, where he hauled himself up onto a shallow ledge so that he could be seen by all eyes.

He waited until the expectation in the air was almost unbearable. He cast an eye about all the gathered forms, grandly cleared his throat, and spoke.

"Lutra!" Shimmer began, pushing himself upright onto his haunches.

"As your Queen, it is my job not only to welcome you to the Festival, but to ensure that it keeps alive the spirit of who we are, and what we stand for."

Beyond the waterfall, the gleaming red-gold twilight began to dim, and rich blue shadows crept slowly over the village.

"Our Festival of Love isn't just a time for games and festivities. As you all know... love can take many forms. It can be familial. It can be friendly. It can be a bond that lasts a lifetime, or it can be fleeting. But we gather here tonight to celebrate our love for one another, no matter the form it takes. We celebrate the love of your mother or your brother, the love of your partner or yourself... and the love for those we have lost."

Shimmer paused, allowing the Lutra a moment of mourning.

"We celebrate tonight the love of our home, and our island. We celebrate our love for living and life itself! For we are the Lutra! We are fluid and adaptable, like water! We protect each other, we aid each other, and we keep each other safe. Why? Because that's what love is. Love is love. And no matter what, it is what keeps us strong."

The last echoes of twilight faded into a deep blue. As night fell the laid-out flowers lit up into a rainbow of neon; their light bright enough to see by. Mothers and fathers in the crowd giggled at the looks of awe lighting up their young pups' faces.

"...And with that, let the festival begin!"

Voices of the assembled Lutra rose up into a booming cheer. Those gathered began to dance and play, diving into the waterfall pool and chasing one another around the plateau.

As voices raised in raucous harmony they finally formed into a single crowd, and then surged down into the village as one, following the path of flowers in a parade of extravagantly decorated bodies.

Shimmer's eyes lit up with joy as he hopped down from his ledge to meet his son. Any reservations Indigo had were lost as they joined in the parade, and he spent the night playing, laughing, and feasting until the morning sun rose anew.

Chapter 2

The Calamity

For Sienna, the next few weeks blurred together. He couldn't remember the last time he'd been able to move without a lancing pain in his muscles, or get up on a morning without fighting against the stiffness in his joints.

And Caldera? As always, she soldiered on. Never did his mother show any sign that she was in pain, although her motions grew stiffer by the day, and there were some mornings that Sienna even had to help her up the mountainside.

Those already rare moments of solace that allowed Sienna a chance to watch the sunset or dream of greater things, became fewer and farther between.

He'd almost forgotten what it was like to hope.

With almost robotic monotony, Sienna retrieved the season's meagre harvest, uprooting the bitterbud stems with a gentle muzzle and then overturning the soil so that it could be freshly sowed.

The small, furry bodies of nibblets fled with frantic hopping motions as he and his mother pushed through the towering stems. The little pests were a terrible problem when it came to farming on the slopes; and it was their breeding season. Luckily though, they rarely hung around when the much larger Ailura approached.

One was brave enough to face him, tottering threateningly from side to side on short, twiggy legs. Its wrinkled muzzle parted to bare tiny, but sharp, incisors.

It wavered in front of him, a paw-sized ball of anger and fluff, screaming and swaying.

"Shoo," Sienna grumbled, swatting at it with his paw. "Go on. Git."

The nibblet waited until Sienna moved closer and then, seemingly intimidated, it let out a final squawk and hopped away. Sienna shook his head, and continued working without further complaint from the nibblets.

Some time later, he heard a rustle in the greenery ahead of him, and his mother shouldered through, carrying the two broken halves of a metal tool.

"I need this fixed before we finish the harvest," Caldera said drily, dropping it at his paws with a clang. "If Blaze isn't back yet, take it to old Rusty."

Numbly, Sienna nodded.

Soon he was on his way down to the village, carrying the metal in his mouth.

This time, though, it wasn't even a chance to see Blaze.

After their discussion a few weeks back, Sienna had rarely had the chance to visit his friend. More and more often she was somewhere other than her forge, and after a time, he couldn't find her anywhere.

Sienna began to miss her dearly; forced to visit other blacksmiths that lived and worked in their billowing towers. Sienna could only hope that she'd had a breakthrough. The other blacksmiths could get things done, it was true, but he couldn't help feeling that their work had half the heart Blaze's did.

And then... they, too, began to disappear. Soon there were only a few smiths still working, most of them old, with greying muzzles.

Sienna reached Rusty's forge some time later, offering

his mother's tool without much in the way of an introduction.

With professional silence, the old, half-tailed smith got to work.

"Rusty? Do you know what happened to the others?" Sienna asked, after a prolonged period of silence while the old creature worked his craft, slowly yet diligently.

"Eh? What's that, youngun? The other smithies?" the old one said, turning slowly towards Sienna. His yellow eyes shone in the firelight. "Mmmh. I can't say for certain."

"Well, can you guess?" Sienna asked hopefully.

The old blacksmith laughed hoarsely. "Oh, yes. My guess is that they followed the bright young lass down to the sea."

"Bright young lass? Do you mean... Blaze?"

"Perhaps, yes. A real spitfire, she was. Lovely dark fur, and a real eye for detail, too. Does that sound right?"

Sienna nodded. "That's her."

"Mmhm. Well, she came around all the smithies. Said there's somethin' we had to see. Somethin' that could change our lives, if we could only help to make it work."

"I see. Why didn't you go, then?"

Rusty huffed and looked away. "Hah! I don't have enough life left in me to change it. These old bones wouldn't even make it down to the cove."

Sienna nodded. "I see."

The pair fell into silence, and Sienna into thought. Although his bones still ached and his eyes still prickled with exhaustion, Sienna couldn't help a slight twinge of hope raising the fur along his spine.

Could it really be true?

But... then, if Blaze was gathering the blacksmiths, why hadn't he known? Was she hiding it from him?

No... of course she wasn't. Sienna was the closest friend Blaze had, and Blaze was Sienna's. They told each other everything, they had since they were cubs.

Despite trying to reassure himself, Sienna still felt cold fingers of dread closing in around his stomach.

But… what if she had? Would she really do that? After all this… would she leave him behind?

The longer he sat still, the harder it became. His tail curled with discomfort.

Finally he looked up towards Rusty, working away by the fire. "How long do you think you'll be?" he asked.

"Oh, another hour. Maybe two. Plenty of time for a nap."

"…Or a walk down the cove?"

Rusty's half-tail twitched as he turned to look at Sienna. "Yes. Or that. Whatever kindles your fire." There was a mischievous twinkle in his eye. "Don't worry, I won't tell your mother."

"Alright, I won't be long."

"Burn Bright, youngun."

As always after the Festival, Indigo's life had returned to its usual tedium. His time was mostly spent scavenging for rocks and pretty things from the rich reefs around the island, fishing food for his fathers, and of course basking in the warm, early summer sun.

His favourite finds, he had woven into a lovely necklace of seashells and pearls, threaded along a simple rope of seaweed that hung around his neck. Of course, it was far less formal and far more convenient than his festival chain. Easy enough to swim in too, provided it didn't come undone in the current.

It was an easy life, and Indigo couldn't complain; for many, this was the time of year when things got busiest. Pups were born, lovers were courting, and even Indigo's fathers were caught up in their yearly whirlwind of romance.

But for Indigo, summer tended to be insufferably boring.

Today, he lounged on the beach, letting the sun's rays

soak through his hide and the soft sand caress his belly. Having caught enough food to satiate both fathers and himself, Indigo had left them to their business and gone to relax.

Perhaps romancing was something Indigo should have been doing as well; but he liked the idea of relaxing far more. For one thing, despite stories of a wild and carefree youth, Shimmer rarely left the village except to hunt food for his partner, and Indigo didn't think he wanted that to happen to him… at least not so soon.

And for another, who would he even *want* to take as a mate?

All of his closest friends had paired up last summer, and that left only a few young Lutra that Indigo really got along with. There was the lovely Azure, who always won when they played tag or bubbleberry, and the handsome Ripple, who was quite good at singing, and the chubby Cobalt, who knew exactly which herbs did what.

They had played together plenty over the years, but Indigo didn't think it was *love*. Perhaps they were just as disinterested in the idea as he was.

The sun growing too hot for him, Indigo rolled over on his back, exposing his belly and resting his paws on his chest. With the soothing lap of the waves as a lullaby and the gentle trilling of creatures in the foliage to assure him that he was safe, Indigo yawned. He didn't need to make a decision for a long time yet. Really, he didn't need to make a decision at all. No, Indigo was free to enjoy life, and he was going to do just that.

With the sun warming his fur and the sand soft against his back, the songs of Indigna playing in his ears, Indigo drifted off into peaceful slumber.

By the time he reached the top of the cliff overlooking the cove, Sienna could already see shapes moving far below him. From all the way up here, they looked as small as insects. Once the Ailura had started descending the cliff, though, he found that he couldn't look down.

Landslides had made the path into the cove difficult to navigate. A single misstep could send Sienna plummeting down the rockface, potentially to his death. More than once small pebbles skittered down the cliff face, making his heart pound. No doubt the sound of falling rocks drew attention from the gathering of Ailura below, but by the time he reached the rocky shore they had returned to their prior tasks.

Sienna recognized the assembled Ailura as the island's blacksmiths, or most of them, anyway. There must have been around fifteen of them, some carrying bleached stones and scraps of metal. A group of five Ailura clustered by the water, bustling amongst themselves and surrounding something floating in the shallows.

But before he could fully take in the sight, a familiar voice caught Sienna's attention.

"Flint, bring that rock over here. Flicker, go get more reeds. Scorch, get over here, I'm gonna need you to– Sienna, is that you?"

Sienna's fluffy ears turned to the sound of his name. He froze, his blood momentarily running cold, as he realized that he had no idea what he wanted to say.

He didn't have much time to dwell on it, though, as the impact of something large and fluffy sent him sprawling to the ground, winded.

Sienna thought at first that Blaze was chasing him away; that she and the others would send him turning tail and fleeing back to the village. But, when Sienna rolled over and looked into her face, he saw that her eyes were bright with joy.

Seeing that, any frustration following her disappearance melted away.

An Ailura with mottled patches stood by, watching awkwardly as he awaited Blaze's command. "Err, miss Blaze? What did you want me to do again?"

"Oh, Scorch! Ah, yes..." Blaze took a moment to

consider, looking over the young blacksmith with a keen eye. "Would you go and find me more driftwood?"

Scorch dipped his head, striped tail waving, before hurrying off.

Blaze turned back towards Sienna.

"What are you doing here? Shouldn't you be helping your– ah, thank you, Flint."

Blaze was cut off, yet again, as a slate-grey smith dropped a large chunk of rock at her paws.

Sienna paused impatiently as the other smith bowed his head and then turned tail. He waited until he was gone before finally answering Blaze's questions.

"I had to go get the stick repaired again–... a few times, actually... but Rusty is nowhere near as quick as you were. He said you were doing something down in the cove, so I decided to take a walk down to see you."

"Sounds about right."

"Now what are *you* doing here?"

Sienna watched her face light up, as he knew it would. "Come on, I'll show you."

Blaze stooped to pick up the stone that Flint had brought her and gestured with her tail to Sienna. Then, with it waving like a banner out behind her, she began to move towards the crowd of blacksmiths. After a moment's hesitation, Sienna followed. He was amazed to see how the crowd parted around her, allowing her passage to the water's edge.

His gaze was drawn, again, to the seemingly-ordinary grey stones that she – along with many of the others – were carrying.

"What are those for?" Sienna murmured.

Blaze turned back. After a moment's consideration, she put hers down. "Those little rocks are what's gonna help us get away from this place," she said. "You aren't gonna believe me, but they *float*."

"They *float*?"

"Yes. *Float*."

That couldn't be right. Rocks didn't *float*! Throw a pebble into the sea and it wouldn't. Push a boulder off a cliff and it shouldn't. What made these ordinary stones so special?

So intent was Sienna on keeping up with Blaze that he didn't notice the seawater swelling up the beach until it soaked the tips of his toes.

Fear gripped him in that moment, and he jumped back, springing away from the water. Although he had only touched it for an instant, his paws already felt heavier than lead. With fur dense enough to be fireproof, the Ailura couldn't swim if they tried.

Blaze continued, though, until her paws were submerged to the ankles. She must have done this a thousand times before to be this unafraid.

Sienna watched her with gobsmacked admiration as she raised her forepaws out of the water and hauled herself up onto... something.

He didn't quite know how to describe it, really. Blaze's project was... well, driftwood, mostly. It was a platform, cobbled together out of bleached logs and branches haphazardly tied together with plant fibres. There were a lot of the rocks too, and they did indeed float. They kept the raft stabilized when there wasn't enough driftwood to keep it surfaced, and if the raft did happen to dip under the weight of the Ailura, the stones would pull the platform back up. The deck was composed entirely of rocks as well, bound together with rivulets of molten metal. Some sort of metal rod stuck out of the rear of the floating contraption, curved at the end. A steering mechanism?

It was a crude, small, ugly looking little raft, but that wasn't important.

What was important on the other hand, was...

"Does it work?" Sienna asked.

Blaze looked down at him, perched on top of the raft with her tail flowing in a sea breeze. "Well... we haven't tested it yet. But the design is sound."

"Ah, right. Well... There's time for that, yet."

Looking down further along the beach Sienna could see more rafts, some finished like this one, others only half done. They looked as though they *might* be able to hold five Ailura in each, maybe more if they squeezed. But that wasn't many.

Blaze nodded eagerly. "Yes, indeed. And we're so close now, I can feel it."

For the first time in weeks, Sienna felt a smile growing on his face. But, as the moments passed, that smile slowly died. "Blaze... Why didn't you tell me about all this?"

"It just all came about so quickly. After talking to you, I realized that I need to make this happen, or no-one will. I think I got so wrapped up in this that everything else just seemed... less important." Blaze's expression mellowed. "Are you upset?"

"No, no... of course not. I just..." Sienna paused, trailing off. Blaze's company had been a release from the tedium of harsh mountain life and the bone-headed stubbornness of his mother. He had thought... up until now... that she had felt the same. He finally looked away.

He looked up again as Blaze jumped down from the raft, causing a splash that sent droplets splattering onto his fur. Sienna shook himself, reeling. He felt her snout nosing gently into his cheek. And then her muzzle tickled his ear as she whispered for only him to hear.

"If... If it makes you feel any better, sometimes when things got tough, it was the thought of you seeing it finished that kept me going."

Sienna felt the tips of his ears burn. And it did help.

The words warmed him to the very core.

"If anyone can do this," Sienna said softly. "It's you."

Blaze nodded, her eyes shining.

Sienna glanced upwards towards the sun, checking its position in the sky. He realized that it was almost sundown. The Mothering Moon was beginning to rise again. It had been an hour.

Damn.

"Listen, I'd best be going. Mother will gut me if I don't get the lever-stick back to her in time."

Blaze nodded. "Say hello to Caldera for me."

"Will do. Burn Bright."

"Burn Bright."

Sienna began to move towards the path back up the cliff face. He climbed upwards, feeling Blaze's eyes following him, until when he looked back the blacksmiths were no bigger than pebbles. There was still a way to go.

As he paused for breath, a thrumming vibration flooded up through his paws. His stomach dropped. He had to get to the top.

He scrabbled faster than he'd ever hoped to scale the treacherous path.

As the terrain levelled out, the peak of the great mountain came slowly into view. He was almost there.

And then the quake truly began. Sienna fought for a hold as the cliff face tried to buck him off. The ground beneath his hindpaws fell away, leaving them dangling over nothingness. He struggled to keep a hold, hearing a distant voice cry out.

"Sienna!"

…and then the cliff face fell away. Earth, rocks, and rubble fell, hanging level with him as though in stasis. Those moments seemed to last a lifetime.

He cast one last desperate glance up.

The last thing he saw was part of the mountainside crashing down in a wave towards the village…

And then Sienna was falling, too. He hit the ground sideways, pain deafening him to everything else. He was vaguely aware of the cliff face coming down inches from his tail.

His side felt warm and wet, his breaths struggling.

He could taste metal.

As blurred vision came back into focus, Sienna caught sight of Blaze's frantic expression. He shrugged it off, and staggered to his paws, sending a lancing pain down one side of his body. Sienna gritted his teeth, and limped forward. He threw himself at the collapsed rock wall, struggling to climb back up.

A sharp pain in his tail brought him back to the present,

and he yelped, turning back, to see that Blaze had grabbed it, yanking him roughly back down onto the ground.

"Stop that! We need to get a healer."

"No! I can't stay!"

"Why not? Your mother will understand—..."

The fire in Sienna's heart died down, smothered by sudden cold.

His mother. She was up on the slopes.

The image of an avalanche of rock and stone replayed in his mind. His throat closed up. "The mountain... The mountain has... the village..." Sienna couldn't get the words out, but he saw the expressions change from confusion to horror around him. Sienna once again mounted the cliff face. This time Blaze didn't try to stop him.

"I have to go back for her."

A low and reverberating boom jolted Indigo awake, whiskers twitching, frozen. The sound quickly faded, but its echoes lingered, carrying across the sea.

Intrigued, Indigo looked out at the horizon, towards where the sound had come from. He stared out there, frozen, hardly daring to breathe for the longest minute. Just as he thought nothing else was going to happen, a plume of smoke began rising above the horizon like an ominous storm cloud.

It rose in a straight pillar upwards before dissipating high in the sky, unlike any storm he'd ever known.

Indigo watched, fascinated. Whatever was making the smoke and the sound, had to be very big and far away, miles perhaps, across the open ocean. Logic battled with curiosity. His fathers had always warned him against chasing storm clouds. On the other hand, Indigo had time on his paws and had been aching for something to do.

With the elegance of a breaking wave, the Lutra slid into the sea leaving barely a ripple. The chill of the water soothed his sun-warmed body, and he shivered slightly. Once he was afloat, he let the current carry him away from the shore, his nose and whiskers just barely poking out above the water.

Soon the island of Indigna was just a distant shadow on the horizon.

With a hunger for adventure powering him forward, Indigo's head finally ducked under the ocean waves, and he disappeared with a splash.

What had been a pleasant golden dusk had quickly become as dark as a winter storm. The air was thick with ash, and choking with sulphur. When Sienna reached the village, dozens of horrified faces stared up at the mountain.

Turning to look for himself, Sienna saw it belching thick black smoke into the sky, choking the sun and blotting out the moons.

Sobbing Ailura tried desperately to rescue trapped family members from piles of rubble and collapsed homes.

This was all that remained of their once-proud race.

The rock-sliders that had also called this place home had disappeared as well, presumably having hidden themselves under boulders or in shadowed corners in a desperate bid to escape the commotion.

"Get to the cove!" Sienna yelled above the din. Above the crying voices and rapidly spreading panic, Sienna didn't think he was heard. "Everyone, listen to me! You have to go!"

One or two frightened faces turned towards him.

Despite his words of guidance, his desperate call to evacuate, Sienna didn't think that the rafts would be enough. And even then, he relied on the Blacksmiths.

What if they simply hopped on board the rafts and deserted? But that didn't matter, not right now.

Another voice chimed in, deep and clear.

"To the cove! The cove!"

Sienna turned, and against the smoke and dark shadows picked out the gleam of red eyes and dark fur. Blaze had arrived; to either side of her stood two other blacksmiths. Sienna recognized the young, bright-eyed Scorch, along with the burly, slate-grey Flint.

Blaze offered Sienna a nod, before turning towards her smiths.

She said nothing, but her eyes had spoken for her.

Go help your mother.

Leaving the village to organize themselves, Sienna turned tail. Despite the sharp pains shooting through him, he tore up the mountain with as much haste as his wounded body would allow.

Instinct carried Sienna up the mountain path that he knew so well, now scattered with boulders and rubble, the path fragmented. He scrambled over debris blocking the path and hurdled gaps where it had fallen away.

Grey flakes of ash fell like snow from the heavens.

As he neared the farm, his breaths were ragged and rasping, his shoulders heaving. He slowed to a halt as he finally came to the plateau where he and his mother had grown their crops. Boulders were haphazardly scattered around the part of the field that survived. The rest had come loose and went careening down the mountain slopes. Rubble had piled onto their scraggly crops. Only a tiny part of the plateau was still traversable.

And he could not see Caldera anywhere.

His heart in his mouth, nausea rising in his belly, Sienna picked his way over to the edge of the cliff and looked down.

He could see the remnants of the landslide, rocks and rubble scattering the mountain slopes. But no Caldera.

He could see the village, too, almost empty now except for the three figures of Blaze, Scorch and Flint. A line of Ailura moved slowly down towards the Cove. Sienna came to the chilling realization that there were not many left.

Sienna returned to his search with paws that felt as heavy as lead. He picked his way around fallen rocks and dug into piles of dust and debris.

"Mother!" he called out, breathless with despair. "Caldera!"

He dug into a drift that collapsed shortly after. Still he did not give up. Finally, he rolled aside a boulder, and found a patch of beige fur, buried under a light covering of rubble.

Hardly daring to breathe, Sienna dug into the debris, nudging fragments of rock and the scraggly remains of crops off her. He unveiled her ears and nose, and her forepaws, and finally her haunches, caked with blood. He nosed at her throat, her neck, her side.

She was still warm.

"Mother...!"

Caldera choked, sending a puff of grey dust spiralling around her muzzle, and a spray of red onto the ground.

"Sienna..." Her voice was faint, hoarse. "For once... I'm glad you dawdled..."

Sienna didn't know whether to laugh or cry. His eyes prickled, although whether it was with tears or the sulphur in the air, he couldn't quite tell.

"Come on... We're going to get you out of here, and then we're leaving this island."

He nudged at her side, and she heaved a breath, shifting her forepaws, but didn't make any effort to get up. Instead, Sienna nudged under her belly, trying to lift her.

"It... won't work."

"Why not?"

"The rocks were crushing. I... can't feel my back legs. Even if we survive, I'll be no use to you."

"Mother, I don't *care* if you're of use to me. I'm getting you off this island."

"No... Sienna... you'll die trying."

"I don't care." Sienna's vision blurred, and this time he knew it was tears.

"Sienna…"

"I'm not leaving you here."

"Son… my time has been long overdue. Whenever we worked these fields, I've felt the years creeping in. I'm old, Sienna. Older than you know. Even if you saved me now, I wouldn't live another moon."

"No… That's not true."

"It is true. And you know it is…. I didn't raise a fool."

Sienna's throat closed up, and he couldn't find any words. Those that he thought of, the ones he knew he needed to say, hurt too much.

And so, he buried his face into the fur of her belly, as though he was still a nursing pup. He felt her breaths heaving, savoured the softness of her fur. Even as he sensed the ground begin to tremble beneath his paws, Sienna stayed exactly where he was.

"You need to go, Sienna. We both do."

Caldera's voice, faint and soft, held a gentleness that he didn't think he'd heard in years.

Her breaths evened, and then, finally, trailed off.

In time, her warmth began to fade. The blood from her wounds ceased to flow. When Sienna finally raised his head to look at her one last time, he thought she looked younger than she had in years.

Grey flakes of ash began to fall around him, unsettlingly serene, some coming to rest on her golden fur.

Soon, she would be buried.

The tremors from the earth intensified as the mountain began to growl. Although Sienna knew he didn't want to leave, the air was growing thicker, and in the end he managed to tear himself away.

Heart aching, breaths sobbing, he staggered back down the mountain path. It was as though time stood still. The journey felt like it took an eternity, but he made it down to the rafts.

A few solitary Ailura milled around on the shore. Sienna did not look at them, but a warmth at his side ushered him away from the shore and into the water, before nudging him onto a raft.

He soon felt the world tilting, heard panicked voices crying out, the sound of wood straining. But it held. And then they were moving.

The last thing he would remember of that day was seeing the distant mountain run red with rivulets of fire.

As he swam across the open ocean, Indigo found his mind drawn back to the stories of his elders. In the days of his puphood, he had spent hours listening to silver-whiskered old paddlers rambling about tentacled horrors, monstrous creatures, and ancient leviathans that supposedly lived in the depths of the sea.

And up until now, that was all they had been. Stories. As he aged, Indigo had come to dismiss the terrifying beasts of the deep as nothing more than rumour and folklore.

But now, as fractured sunlight filtered down from above and a terrifying abyss lay below, with no seabed in sight... Indigo began to wonder just what lurked all those leagues below. Nothing swam out here; only occasionally did he see the fleeting glimmer of life in the distance. There was no seaweed or kelp, coral or rocks. The water was beautiful, crystal clear, featureless.

If something were to find him out here, Indigo would have nowhere to hide. His only company was his wild imagination and the tales it spun from the dark.

Finally, just as Indigo began to fear that he should turn back, the seabed rose up beneath him until it was only a few hundred yards away, littered with boulders and seagrass.

The water began to grow dark and cold, as though the sun was going down, but Indigo knew for a fact that there were hours yet to wait.

Eventually, when Indigo rose to the surface, he could

no longer see the island of Indigna. The smoke had formed into a massive cloud above the sea that plunged the world into darkness. He could see the source, now; an island, and a mountain peak belching fire into the sky. A film of ash had settled on the surface of the sea; its waters tasted bitter to his tongue.

The smoke was heavy on his lungs as he breathed air, so Indigo ducked his head beneath the water to gulp oxygen into his gills. When he popped up again, Indigo looked around, treading water among the waves. He had never seen anything like this before.

A small island – barely a broken precipice – rose up out of the water nearby, with crashing waves foaming around its base. Eager for a rest, Indigo paddled towards it, finally hauling himself up onto jagged grey stone. Climbing up onto the island's peak gave Indigo a much better view of the sea. As he looked around, the Lutra was surprised to see that this island appeared to be one of many forsaken rocks rising up out of the sea. A stunted tree had once grown upon this one, though, gnarled and bleached from the waves.

What on earth is a tree doing here, so far from the land? Indigo found himself wondering, as he allowed himself a moment for the strength to filter back into his limbs. As he looked out over the other islands, though, he realized that this tree was not alone. Petrified trunks rose from the other islands as well.

Strange.

But, even stranger were the things bobbing in the waves just beyond a formation of broken rocks, drifting gradually into view. Indigo's curiosity was, once again, piqued.

He watched them floating on the ocean for a while until his lungs grew tight, and then eased himself back towards the water, sliding in amongst the waves with the slightest splash.

Then, with only the slightest amount of hesitation and even less fear, he set off towards the floating shapes.

As Indigo drew near, he became acutely aware of how odd these things actually were. Indigo swam beneath them and saw that they were made of driftwood and stone. A spiderweb of cracks between these materials were plugged with a strange, dark, shimmery substance that looked as cold as it felt to his paws.

As he hid in their shadows, he could hear claws scraping against the topside. And, when he surfaced, Indigo was surprised to hear voices.

Even more surprising, though, was the fact that he understood them. His mind reeling, Indigo tried to figure out how. But he couldn't find an explanation.

Keeping quiet, with only his eyes and ears above the water, Indigo listened as best he could.

"–still. I can't believe we managed to save as many as we did."

"I suppose. But now that we're here, what is there to do? The oars weren't finished. All we can do is turn the rudder and hope for the best."

"The stories say that our ancestors didn't always live on Veramilia. There's got to be something else out there."

"I suppose so. It's just getting there that will be hard."

"With you on board, I think we'll make it."

"You're far too optimistic, Scorch. But thank you."

"…Perhaps Rusty will–…"

A wave washed over Indigo's head, drowning out the voices for a moment. By the time he resurfaced, someone else was speaking.

"–should come see him, Blaze. His wounds aren't terribly severe – a few broken ribs, perhaps – yet he still won't wake."

"Oh no… Thank you, Flint. Is there anything else?"

"He's mumbling in his sleep. Crying out for his mother."

"I always thought old Caldera was unstoppable," said the voice that Indigo now knew was Scorch. "I wonder what happened to her."

"I… I know. Poor Sienna. I think he was the only thing that old flame ever loved."

The voices faded away as the creatures moved to the other side of the raft. In an effort to keep listening, Indigo dived beneath the water, resurfacing on the other side. He was a little further away this time, and when he looked up, he could see them.

Indigo stared.

These creatures were fluffier than anything he'd seen on Indigna. Their coats shone in dusky tones of red, orange and gold as they wandered across the floating islands. Each and every one of them had white or pale muzzles and ears, and tear-track markings down their cheeks. They all had long, striped tails that waved, long and trailing like kelp fronds. One of them was very dark though, almost black, with red eyes. One of them was slate-grey, one mottled red. They peered down at something with rusty-red fur on the deck, but that was all Indigo could make out.

Indigo was so entranced by the unusual creatures, that he lost track of their conversation entirely until the moment the mottled red one looked up, and into his deep blue eyes.

The creature had eyes that were orange like fire, and Indigo found himself suddenly filled with fear.

"What is–?!"

Indigo didn't hear the rest. With a splash, he was gone. He did not resurface again until he was well out at sea, when the island of Veramilia was little more than a jagged silhouette, and Indigna a distant shadow on the horizon.

But Indigo's thoughts lingered there. In his mind's eye he could still see those red creatures on their strange floating platforms.

To his relief, the current carried him most of the way home.

But even then, far away from the refugees, his thoughts kept on sneaking back, his head turning and gaze lingering on the distant pillar of smoke. More than anything else, Indigo remembered the expressions on their faces: a sheer despair the likes of which he had never seen on the face of a Lutra.

Chapter 3

Adrift

"There are creatures on the sea!"

Indigo burst back into the village that evening, exhausted and relieved to be home, but frantic. The town was quiet; empty except for a few tired hunter-gatherers.

Confused faces turned towards him.

"Princess Indigo...? What sort of creatures?" a lilac hunter asked at length, as though afraid of the answer.

"Creatures the colour of stone and fire! Creatures that float on platforms of stone and driftwood! They've come from the place the smoke is coming from!"

"The smoke column? But... that's so far out at sea! How do you know?!"

"I went there! I wanted to see where the smoke was coming from."

"You went there? Didn't your parents ever tell you that curiosity killed the clam?"

"Well, I... that's besides the point! The point is, they're out there floating on the open sea! And we're the only ones who could possibly save them!"

"Creatures of stone and fire?" an old, crackling voice

echoed, slowly, as though she'd only just heard what had been said.

The village healer, Shard, pushed her way out of a nearby den, offering Indigo a frosty glare. She was long and serpentine, mostly white but for a dusting of blue across her muzzle and paws. She might once have been beautiful, if it weren't for her sour expression accentuated by the wicked claw marks across her left eye. By her ruffled whiskers, Indigo knew that he'd just disturbed her nap.

The other Lutra fell into a hushed silence, all gazes fixing on Shard.

"Yes, Shard! They came from an island pouring smoke into the sky! You believe me, don't you?"

The wizened old Lutra's gaze flickered from him to the others gathered, watching her. Of all the elders, she might be the one who'd travelled the furthest in her youth.

Surely she would know?

"–It's impossible. Nothing like that in the world exists. I would know."

Indigo's heart sank. He looked wildly around at the assembled Lutra with thinly-veiled embarrassment, looking for an expression of belief, or even the curiosity that Lutra were known for.

And he saw… hesitation.

"N-no, wait! It is true! I've seen them! I heard them! I… You have to believe me! Not even Shard could have explored every island in the ocean!"

The hunter-gatherers murmured amongst themselves. They had no reason to dismiss his claims entirely. Whiskers lifting with renewed confidence, Indigo straightened up a little taller. "Even if you don't believe me… my point still stands. There are creatures out there on the ocean, with no hope of surviving and nowhere to go. As Princess of the Lutra, it's my duty to change that."

"Well, what do you want us to do?"

"I, er, well… Their platforms can float, but they can't move. I was thinking that we could help to push them to shore."

A long silence answered him.

"All that way?"

"From island to island?"

Indigo realized that he had acted too quickly, and he didn't really have a plan at all. His skin grew hot under his fur.

"Well, I... hadn't thought that far ahead," he admitted. An idea struck him. "My fathers will know what to do."

He bounded off, leaving the Lutra to stare bewilderedly after him, aching for sleep, and yet wondering if they ought to stay awake.

Pain.

It was the first thing to resurface as Sienna's consciousness returned.

His ribs throbbed as he breathed sharp and irregular breaths. His surface wound stung terribly.

He could feel every tickle of the cold sea breeze. The ground beneath his paws was gently rocking, making his stomach turn with nausea as he lay. He could smell salt, blood, and fear.

"Ugh... mother," he half-whispered, his eyes cracking open to amber slits. At first, Sienna was shocked and terrified by the bodies around him, sprawled out or curled into tight, fluffy balls. He sat up, suddenly wide awake. The Ailura gritted his teeth against a sharp stab of pain, narrowing his eyes. As the pain settled, Sienna noticed the slow rising and falling of the others' sides, and realized that they were only sleeping.

Looking around warily, Sienna turned his gaze upwards. Overhead was a rich violet sky, the stars gradually winking out as the morning brightened. The sun was low in the sky, and from its position in the east, it had only just risen. The sky around it was tinted rose-gold. Grey-black clouds hung motionless in an otherwise clear sky, painting a clear pathway towards where they had come. The small cub-moon hung above them at the apex of the sky. His ears pricked, but the world was quiet, other than the gentle lapping of the waves against the side of their raft.

Sienna found the peaceful nature of the scene unnerving. His fur puffed out from head to tail.

His side sang with pain once more as he struggled up onto all four paws and looked around. They were on a raft. The floor of stone and rivulets of metal felt rough against his paws. The silhouette of an Ailura sat by a lever at the other end of the raft, staring out to sea. As he moved over to her, picking his way around and over the other sleeping forms, his paws soaked up a shallow film of water.

Sienna shivered.

The other Ailura did not look up as he drew near. "Blaze? Is that you?"

She looked up sharply, eyes wide.

"Sienna? Oh, thank the Fire, you're awake!" She moved over to touch her nose to his, with all the enthusiasm and relief that Sienna had missed so much in her absence.

But today it brought no comfort.

He did not rise to meet her nudge, and as she withdrew, Sienna turned his gaze out to sea. In the nearer distance, he saw the ramshackle forms of more rafts, some close, some barely specks on the horizon. With nothing holding them together, the rafts were beginning to scatter. Beyond those, he saw the distant shape of a mountain rising from the sea. Their mountain, leaking its last tendrils of smoke.

"What's... What's going on?" Sienna finally asked. "How long have I been out?"

"We escaped Veramilia. You've been out since... Let's see... all of yesterday and a full night. How much do you remember?"

Sienna shrugged.

"I remember... the mountain belching smoke and fire. I remember running for my life. And I remember..." He fell silent, his mouth growing dry.

Loss.

Sienna remembered in a haze what had become of Caldera, of his mother. He remembered her words, her calm stubbornness even in the face of the end.

"...Mother... She didn't... she..." He couldn't finish the sentence, his voice catching on the lump in his throat.

"I know, Sienna."

"...She's still on the island."

"Yes."

They fell silent. Sienna didn't know what to say. What to do. He felt hollowness where there should have been grief. Guilt where there should have been memories.

If only I'd stayed... The thought began, but was left unfinished. Nothing could have stopped the burning mountain or the landslide. Nothing could have stopped the years creeping on.

If he'd been the one to die, Caldera would not have sat and mourned. And if she could have seen him now, she would never have let him sit down and dwell on it. Not when there was work to be done.

Sienna felt his cheeks growing wet with tears, and he shook his head, blinking his blurry eyes until they were clear.

"How many..." his voice came out a croak, and he cleared his throat. "How many did we save?"

Blaze looked out towards the other floating platforms.

"More than I expected," she said. "Most of the village made it onto the rafts. Some are a little heavy, but none of them have sunk, which is good."

Sienna nodded. "And all thanks to you."

Blaze shook her head. "Don't give me all the credit! It was Scorch's idea to evacuate. Flint was a big help when it came to planning..."

Blaze's eyes darted across the sleeping forms, quickly picking out Scorch's mottled red coat, and Flint's slate-grey one, curled protectively around two smaller lumps of fur. And finally, gentle snores rolled out from a curled up lump of faded orange fur. A striped half-tail flicked as Rusty stirred in his dreams.

"There's no need to be humble. If you hadn't rallied the blacksmiths, who knows where we'd be?"

"Dying in fire rather than in water, probably. We're not out of the ocean yet," Blaze reminded him, a frown showing in her brows, and the tilt of her whiskers.

"True. What's the plan, then?"

"Well…" Blaze cleared her throat. "…Don't really have one, can't really make one. The oars weren't finished, so all we can really do is float and hope for the best. And it's not like we can swim to shore."

For the first time, the direness of their situation well and truly set in.

"Any food or purified water?"

"Not one bit. Our intention was to finish the raft and then bring them aboard. But… obviously, that didn't go to plan."

Sienna nodded. "I… I see."

He racked his brain, trying to think of anything that might help. But Caldera's lessons had never prepared him for this. Her life had always been the same, from the day she was born to the day she died. Day after day of monotony, tending to their needs for the next day.

"…Have you seen any land?" Sienna asked eventually. Perhaps if it was close enough, they could figure out a way to get there.

Blaze nodded, and led him to the other side of the raft. They looked out over the sea once more. It took him a moment, but he saw it; a distant smudge of green on the very edge of the horizon.

"We've been floating towards it for some time now. Hopefully we'll keep going that way."

"Okay," Sienna said, sighing in short-lived relief. "At least there's that. Is there anything else I should know?"

Blaze shook her head, then paused, hesitating. "Well…"

"Huh?"

"It's not that important, but Scorch thought he saw something in the water."

"What sort of something?"

"I don't know. He said it was watching us as we talked. He said it was long and blue, with white spots. He said it had no ears, and no legs. Like a chubby, furry rock-slider."

"It sounds… gross," Sienna said, trying and failing to imagine it.

Blaze chuckled, leaning in towards his ear to ensure she couldn't be heard. "Don't tell Scorch this, but I think the smoke might have got to him a little."

Despite the situation, and the heaviness of his heart, Sienna felt the joke lift his spirits just a little bit.

"Still, old Rusty believed him," Blaze continued. "You should have seen his face when Scorch brought it up. He looked like he'd seen a ghost."

In time, the other Ailura began to awaken, one by one. Whilst there were a great deal of disgruntled expressions and a fair amount of nervous tension, there were some individuals who displayed a certain kind of cheer reserved for those who had cheated death and survived the impossible.

Sienna couldn't speak for the other rafts which, right now, were drifting further and further away… but on this one at least, there were seven others of his kind.

Scorch, Rusty and Blaze were the three that Sienna knew the best, and then there was Flint, and a couple of cubs under his care.

Needless to say, the raft was quite crowded. The Ailura had to jostle one another just to move around.

Nonetheless, Scorch seemed almost as pleased to see Sienna awake as Blaze had been, despite knowing him only vaguely. Flint simply acknowledged his presence with a nod as he watched, with a wary eye, his cubs play-wrestling.

Some time after the others had risen, Sienna moved

over to Rusty. The old smith heaved himself up onto his paws with considerable effort, and Sienna helped to nudge him upright as best he could.

"Good to see you back in the land of the living, lad," the blacksmith rasped. "And as well mannered as ever."

Whilst the others tried to keep their spirits up and Blaze tried to steer the raft, Sienna spent a lot of his time perched at the edge, staring at the green smudge on the horizon and trying to work out if it was getting closer.

Quietly he thought back to the time he spent on the mountainside, staring out to sea. He wondered if, perhaps, his mother understood now.

Above the boat, flying creatures reeled on wide wings, screeching. All the Ailura watched them warily.

Occasionally one dived steeply, entering the water with barely a splash. Usually they would resurface with something trailing from their jagged jaws, but they did not always reappear. This scared Sienna more than he was willing to admit.

A few times he looked down and saw lights dancing beneath the waves.

And as much as he tried to peer down through the waves and guess at what they belonged to, the answer always seemed to evade him.

Once his attention was drawn to a shape moving beneath the waves. It wasn't large, and it was hard to pinpoint, but there was something there.

Sienna stared, watching, holding his breath. The shadow grew, taking serpentine form, undulating through the water. He caught sight of pale spotting as its hide neared the surface.

With a faint rush of water and the slightest splash, a whiskered face appeared. Its rounded head shed water and its fur was dry in a moment. Indigo eyes blinked up at him.

The creature's long, blue-grey body moved slowly as the waves lapped about at its dappled form.

"Uh... Hello?" The creature's words broke through his thoughts. Its voice was odd, gentle, and yet heavily accented. Its tone rose and fell like the break of a wave.

Sienna froze, hackles rising as he prepared to jump back. He stared at the face in the water, dumbfounded. Afraid he'd scare the creature away, he spoke in a hushed whisper.

"Did you just–? Blaze? Blaze! Come see this!"

Sienna gestured with a flick of his tail. To his relief, it stayed where it was.

Sienna felt Blaze moving up to stand by his side.

"Oh," she breathed. "It's you."

"You really exist," Sienna said in wonder. "And it... and you... can talk...?"

"–and how'd you learn our language?" Blaze broke in.

"*Your* language?" the thing said. "I want to know how you learned *ours*!"

Before the proceedings could devolve into an argument, Sienna whisked at Blaze's tail with his own, drawing her attention. "Language doesn't matter for now," he said, pointedly. "What does is why you're here. Can you... Can we help you?"

Sienna thought it best to play it safe. If they had something this creature wanted, perhaps it would be easier to earn its favour. He didn't know what this thing was, or what laws it played by, but it swam in the sea. Perhaps they could reach a deal to help bring the Ailura to safety?

"I'm here to help, silly! I don't think there's much you can do for me, especially from tiny islands like these."

Any plans that Sienna had been carefully formulating melted away.

"You... You are?"

"Yes, yes. I've spoken to my village. The Lutra have agreed to help, provided that you get near enough to the shore."

"That's–"

"–Amazing!"

"Thank you, thank you!"

"Don't thank me yet. You need to be nearer to shore, first. Lucky for you, the current pulls from below. You should keep going towards Indigna – that's our island, by the way – for another few days. Can you swim? Paddle, even?"

Sienna answered without hesitation.

"No. Our fur is too thick. It drags us down. We are creatures of fire, not water."

"Hmmm. I see. Then we'll push. The village working together will be enough."

"Will you really be able to get your entire village to help us?"

"Of course!" the creature said, cheerfully. "I have the support of our Queen."

"Oh, thank you. Thank you so much!"

Hearing the commotion, Scorch came up on Sienna's other side, and Rusty beside him. "Hey, that's–"

The curiosity drained from the half-tailed smith's face as he caught sight of the creature looking back at him. But before Sienna could ask, Rusty spoke.

"What's going on?" he asked, voice hoarse.

"We're being saved! By this... by... I'm sorry, what was your name again?"

"Indigo– of the Lutra. Yours?"

"I'm Sienna, and this is–"

"Blaze, Flint, and Scorch, yes? I know," the creature said a little smugly.

Sienna was taken aback. "Well, then, Indigo. Thank you. "

Indigo smiled, whiskers lifting. "No trouble. I'll be back, promise."

"Wait– one last thing. Would you spread the word to the other rafts, as well?"

Indigo appeared to consider for a moment, before offering a brisk nod. And then he was gone, disappearing beneath the waves.

When he didn't reappear, Sienna finally turned towards Rusty. "Hey," he asked curiously. "Is something wrong?"

"Nothing at all," Rusty said, turning his back on Sienna. "I'm simply... surprised, that's all."

"Are you sure? Do you... know that creature?"

"Of course not... I've never known anything beyond

the island. Now if you'll excuse me… all these questions are making my bones ache."

Sienna watched as Rusty slumped down onto the deck, curling his half-tail across his muzzle.

Defeated, curious, and concerned for the elder, Sienna moved back over to Blaze. He listened as she spoke to Scorch, and was unable to help a tiny smile.

"I don't know what you saw earlier," Blaze teased. "…But that thing definitely had ears. And, for that matter, legs."

"Yeah, well… it was gone too quickly last time," protested the young blacksmith. "I only had a second! I think it was scared of me."

"Well, with a face like yours, I'm not surprised!"

Scorch laughed, aghast, but seemed unable to find a sufficient response. In the end, he walked away, leaving her with a defiant flick of his tail. Finally, Sienna was able to rejoin his friend. They sat down together, watching the others as they lay down to rest, play, or admire the view with a renewed sense of composure.

But something was bothering him.

"Do you really think it'll help us?" Sienna murmured into her ear.

"I sure hope so. What other choice do we have?"

Dissatisfied, Sienna shrugged.

The rest of the day passed fairly uneventfully, besides a growing thirst, and the occasional rumble of the Ailura's bellies. The island loomed nearer on the horizon. Perhaps more pressingly though, the next morning brought those bird-like creatures circling again, scales shimmering in the sun. Even as Sienna watched them warily they swooped nearer, beady eyes scanning their rafts.

In the distance, Sienna saw the shadow of a great winged fiend coming in to land on one of the other rafts.

He knew that it was only a matter of time before they set their sights on this one, too.

Luckily, though, the flying creature did not stay long on the other raft, soon taking back to the sky and soaring off overhead with a defiant screech. Sienna could only hope that that was the last he'd see of it.

Sienna quickly moved on with his day, listening to the conversations of the other Ailura as he rested and waited for his wound to heal. He had drifted off into a doze when he was awakened by a commotion, and the shrill cry of a cub.

The sun wasn't much higher in the sky, so he hadn't been asleep for very long.

With a small grunt of effort, Sienna sat up to see what was going on. In a blur of caramel and peach-coloured fur, the two cubs barrelled forward and hid beneath Flint, fleeing from a massive shadow that had fallen on the raft.

The world rocked as a flying creature landed heavily on the deck, furling enormous, leathery wings either side of it. It towered over the Ailura, easily twice their height with the added benefit of a long, twisting neck. Its smooth scales reflected the colour of the sky. Three beady eyes blinked at each fluffy adversary in turn. Finally it clacked a toothy beak, as though warning them to stay back, flaring its wings.

Long, elegant legs carried it forward with slow and terrifying steps, talons rasping against stone and clinking against metal.

All four adult Ailura flinched back, staring at the terrifying seabird with a mixture of wariness and terror.

There was no question about what it wanted from them. The two cubs huddled beneath their adoptive father.

Sienna's heart hammered. He exchanged a glance with Blaze before looking back at the bird.

All of them were speechless, afraid of making a sudden move or sound.

But what could *they* do? This wouldn't be like chasing away the nibblets. This creature was huge, its beak sharp, and its element all around them.

Blaze swayed where she stood, clearly wanting to help, and yet hesitating. Its whole attention was fixed on Sienna; perhaps if he could keep it distracted, she could sneak in, and... and...

After glancing helplessly from Scorch, to Flint, Sienna realized with horror that they all stared back at him, frozen, waiting. He couldn't help but wonder, with a sudden surge of discomfort, why.

He supposed as poorly-suited as his experience was, it was the only experience that meant anything at all. Sienna had spent all of his life keeping starving creatures away from his mother's crops, however small they were. They thought he could use that.

But they were wrong.

Sienna glanced up towards Blaze once more, then offered her a small nod.

His tail swished, flicking behind him. His russet fur prickled upright along his body, and he stepped towards the bird, stiffly. It turned to stare at him, beak slightly parted, middle eye following his tail plume as though hypnotized.

Sienna puffed himself up as big and threatening as he could, then after a moment of thought, rose up onto his hindpaws. They stared one another down, eye to eye.

The creature blinked, cocking its head in a manner that was completely, terrifyingly unafraid.

It hissed softly, as though daring Sienna to make the first move.

The Ailura stole a glance past it, to where Blaze slipped ever closer, lifting her paws high so that they fell softly.

Sienna froze for a second, before moving slightly forward in an effort to intimidate it. The bird, in turn, spread its vast wings.

They stared each other down as the other Ailura watched in fascination.

Suddenly, Sienna heard a quiet splash. A pair of webbed paws appeared at the side of the raft, quickly followed by a whiskered face.

With a terrified squawk and a flurry of wingbeats, the

creature took to the air and flew away. Soon it was no more than a speck above the distant island.

Heart still pounding, Sienna let out a breath that he didn't know he'd been holding, and sank down onto all fours. "Indigo!" Sienna said, moving forward. In his relief, Sienna couldn't find it in himself to question why the terrifying bird was so afraid of him. "Thank goodness!"

The Lutra hauled himself up onto the boat, dragging a large blue fruit along with him. Indigo dropped it onto the deck as he shook the stray droplets from his whiskers. "Never dealt with a Squall before?"

Sienna shook his head. "We've never even seen one before."

"Oooh. Well then, you're lucky. Those beaks hurt, and they can carry off a pup if you're not careful."

"Well then, how do we deal with them?"

"They are big and fearless, but very fragile. Go for the wings, and it will leave you alone. Especially easy in water, you see?"

Indigo glanced out towards the sea before turning back towards Sienna. "They won't be a problem when you get to Indigna, though. They're ocean-hunters, like the Lutra."

Sienna nodded eagerly. After exchanging glances, Scorch and Blaze moved over to speak to Indigo as well, whilst Flint began to console the two cubs with gentle licks of his rough tongue. He noticed Rusty slinking over to be with Flint, offering an extra measure of comfort. Blaze, meanwhile bent down to sniff at the fruit that Indigo had brought them.

Now that he was looking at it closer, Sienna could see that the fruit was slightly more purple than blue, with faint dappled patterns. As he stooped to sniff at it as well, he realized that it didn't smell of anything at all.

"What's this?" Blaze asked, a little suspiciously.

"This is a bubbleberry. They aren't very tasty, but the juice may help with thirst. My father suggested it," Indigo said.

Sienna exchanged glances with Scorch and Blaze.

It was apparent that neither of them were keen on

trying it first. He read the questions in their expressions: *could it be poisonous? What if it tastes bad?*

In truth, Sienna shared the same sentiments. Like them, he had subsisted on a diet of nothing but bitterbud and the occasional sweet sugarstem since he had first been weaned from his mother's milk.

None of them had ever tasted anything else, much less from another land.

"Have you ever eaten them?" Sienna asked Indigo.

"There are usually better things to eat, but sometimes, when there is nothing else. Our kind usually uses them for games. They float and bounce very nicely."

Sienna heard Blaze breathe in, about to speak, but he interrupted her. "I'll try it," he said, abruptly. He feared for his best friend, and as the wounded one, Sienna needed moisture the most of all of them. Having failed to chase away the bird on his own, he may as well try to make up for it.

Indigo chuckled. "There's no need to treat it like a gamble. It's only a fruit."

Sienna stepped forwards, nosing at the skin of the fruit with interest. It was smooth.

A moment later, Sienna gently bit into its skin and peeled off a strip of the outer layer. He took a bite of the soft flesh within. It was wet, bland, and slightly tangy. Its cold flesh soothed his throat as he swallowed, and it felt like the best thing he had ever eaten.

"Mmmm..." Sienna mumbled, through a mouthful of bubbleberry.

"How is it?" Blaze asked, eagerly.

Sienna's answer was to go in for another mouthful. After that he stopped and waited for a while, licking the juice from his whiskers. "...Not poisonous," he finally decided, with another lick of his muzzle. "And delicious."

Their faces lit up.

"See? I told you!" Indigo trilled.

The Ailura took it upon themselves then, to work out who should eat next. The fruit wasn't going to be enough for a feast, of course, but their kind was used to living on rations.

The cubs, it was decided, would eat first, and then Blaze, and finally Scorch and Flint. Only Rusty refused to touch it. By the time everyone had had two or three mouthfuls each, the fruit was little more than a hollow, leathery husk. This was soon devoured as well. When the sun reached its peak, it was time for Indigo to leave once more.

"I'll take bubbleberries to the other platforms, too," Indigo reassured Sienna. "Then they can eat."

"Thank you, Indigo," Sienna said.

"Not a problem, not a problem. Thank me when you get to shore."

"When will that be?"

Indigo looked out towards the island.

"...Two days. Then you'll be in reach, I'd say. Your floating islands are quite slow in the current."

"And then your kind will push us to shore?" remembered Blaze.

"Yes, that's right."

"And... then what?"

"And then... Hrmm. I suppose then you can make your own village. I'm sure, though, that the Queen wouldn't object to a few guests for a day or two. Our village is very large, and very beautiful."

At this, Rusty looked up.

"...Is it underwater?" Sienna asked, quite unable to imagine what a Lutra village would look like.

"No, no... well... sort-of, but there are back ways. To escape floods and the like. It's in a tight curve of the river mouth, where a stream splits off. Water flows through the village, but it is not underwater."

"I see," Sienna murmured, fascinated but wary.

"We'll look forward to it, then," Blaze added.

Indigo dipped his head, slid into the water and was gone.

That evening, Indigo hauled himself ashore and waddled up the path to the village. His lean muscles cramped, his eyelids drooped, and his neck was aching from hauling bubbleberries across the ocean's surface. He didn't think he'd ever worked so hard in his entire life.

Indigo began to wonder if rescuing the Ailura was really worth it.

They were a terribly suspicious lot, who seemed like they'd never seen a day of fun in their lives. That being said, each time Indigo visited them, they were awfully thankful. Their wary expressions had seemed to ease after they ascertained that the bubbleberries weren't poisonous.

As he entered the village, the shapes of Lutra moved on their usual evening routines. They didn't pay him much heed, but offered a cheerful nod or wiggle of their whiskers as they passed.

"How's the rescuing going, Princess?" asked one as Indigo passed him by.

Indigo paused, looking up. A sky-blue Lutra looked back at him. He had no markings, except for a faint sprinkling of dark blue across his haunches.

"Oh, hey Ripple. It's… going well, I think. I brought them bubbleberries to eat, and they seemed to like that."

"Ew, bubbleberries? Are you trying to put them off ever getting here?"

"It was my father's idea. He thought they might be thirsty, and most things can't drink seawater. Besides, they seemed to like them."

"If you say so. Are you heading back to the waterfall cave?"

"Yeah… I'm too tired to do anything else. Why?"

"Might wanna get there fast. I saw Shard heading that way earlier. I think she was going to give the Queen an earful about you."

Indigo's heart sank.

"Alright, then. I'll keep that in mind. Thanks, Ripple."

"Later, Princess."

Indigo continued climbing up the path towards the waterfall, until he could pick out two voices above its roar. As he drew nearer, he realized that Ripple was right. The lilac form of his father stood, noble and shimmering with pearls, facing the snowy white Lutra, who coiled like a pythos ready to spit venom.

Indigo hung back, not out of sight, but just far enough away that they might not notice him.

"–that impudent child, Shimmer. He'll bring death upon us all by bringing those creatures here." Shard was saying, her tone icy.

"Those creatures are helpless and alone in the world. I trust my son's judgement in saving them," Shimmer said.

"So you agree with the child?"

"As I've said, Shard... he is not a *child*. And if we don't bring them to Indigna, they won't survive."

"And that matters to us, how?"

"Because we are the Lutra. We are creatures of open minds and hearts. If these creatures bring negative forces with them, then we will deal with that later."

Indigo thought that his father glanced his way, just for a moment. Their eyes met in that fleeting instant, and Indigo relaxed.

"Just wait until the *Queen*–..."

"I am your Queen, Shard. I just wish you would act like it."

Indigo didn't think he'd ever heard Shimmer speak so coldly.

"You? A queen? Tshh," Shard hissed air through her teeth. "You are *bonded* to the Queen, that's all."

Shimmer's gaze hardened in a way that was seldom seen.

"It was Tide's *choice* to relinquish his title to me. If he wants it back, then the option is always there."

"Have you even *spoken* to him about this matter?"

"Yes, I have."

"And?"

"He agrees with me. With our son."

Shimmer gave a small nod towards Indigo. Shard, finally seeming to notice that he was there, whipped around, her eyes like fragments of ice.

Indigo shivered slightly at the sight of her narrowed eyes crinkling her jagged scar.

"This is a mistake," the old Lutra said, speaking to both of them now. "They will hate us. They will drive us out. That's just how other creatures *are*. They won't see us as anything more than monsters."

"Well, we don't see them as monsters," Indigo said.

"Because you are Lutra. A naive Lutra, but Lutra. But they – these creatures – will not be so open-minded."

"We shall see," Shimmer said.

"I suppose we will," Shard said coldly. "I'll see you around, one hopes."

"Farewell, *mother*," Shimmer answered with uncharacteristic venom. Indigo flinched.

The scarred old Lutra stalked away. Indigo watched her retreat until she was long gone, both father and son falling silent.

Finally, Shimmer spoke.

"I'm really sorry about that."

Indigo didn't quite know how to answer. "It's... okay, Pa. What do you think is her problem?"

Shimmer shook his head, a bewildered expression on his face. When he spoke, his effort to change the subject was painfully obvious.

"How's the rescuing going?"

"It's going well," Indigo said. "Very well, in fact. But I think I need tomorrow off."

Shimmer chuckled, shaking his head. "Off?" he asked, as though the thought amused him.

"Yes. Off."

"Will the Ailura be okay on their own?"

Uncertain what answer Shimmer was looking for, Indigo shrugged. "I gave them bubbleberries today, so they shouldn't starve. I taught them to deal with the Squall, too. And, the day after tomorrow they should be within reach of the island. They won't be alone for long."

"Sounds like you've got everything taken care of, then. Well done," Shimmer said.

Indigo felt the praise warm him to the tips of his paws.

"...But, surely a quick swim out there to check on them tomorrow couldn't hurt, right?"

Indigo grunted. "I suppose."

"...First, though, you should get some rest. You look exhausted."

Indigo relaxed slightly, offering a halfhearted smile. "I am," he admitted.

"Go on, then."

Indigo nodded, taking the words as a farewell. He began to waddle around the waterfall, but as he did, he heard his father's voice call after him.

"Son?"

Indigo halted, turning back towards his father.

"I'm proud of you."

"Thanks, Pa."

Indigo gave his father one last nod, before hopping onto the waterfall lift.

He jumped off at the cave mouth and stumbled through to his sleeping chamber. He collapsed in a heap in the corner, and before he could even acknowledge the blessed relief of soft moss beneath his belly, he was asleep.

The next day advanced into noon, and the island of Indigna loomed closer and closer. The rafts rocked nauseatingly as they drifted nearer to land. The Ailura were attacked twice more by Squall careening out of the sky and onto the deck but after Sienna managed to toss one overboard, breaking its wing in the process, the creatures bothered them no more.

By evening, Blaze's raft was almost within reach of its

shores, a day earlier than Indigo had anticipated.

And yet still, the Lutra did not return.

Unrest brewed among the small group of Ailura confined to the raft, watching the lushly forested shores drift by less than a hundred yards away.

They were going to miss it.

Sienna perched on the edge of the raft as the sun began to set, as though preparing to jump overboard. But he knew that he would drown if he tried.

"Where do you think he is?" Scorch asked anxiously.

"He must have misjudged. We're supposed to be in reach tomorrow, not tonight," Flint said.

"Then... what do we do? He wouldn't just leave us, would he?"

"I don't know, Scorch. We barely know him."

Sienna listened to the exchange in silence, thinking, and worrying. The tip of his tail flicked nervously.

"But if... if we're in reach today, then... where will we be tomorrow?"

They had no answer. The only sounds were the gentle lapping of the waves against the boat and the wind rushing through the distant leaves. Sienna wobbled on the raft's edge, and stepped back as it rocked. It was changing direction.

Sienna looked to shore. "Look," he said, restlessly. "There's the mouth of the river. Indigo mentioned it. The village is close."

The others followed his gaze.

"So... the current..." Blaze trailed off. Her crimson eyes met Sienna's. "We have to get to shore."

"How?" Scorch asked, his voice high with despair. Flint's two cubs whimpered, softly.

Blaze had no answer.

Sienna glanced around wildly. He caught sight of one of the driftwood logs that made up the raft's foundations, its twisting shape still clearly visible. It even had a worn branch or two left...

Sienna bounded over to one of the remaining branches and grasped it in his jaws. Fastening his teeth into the wood and ignoring the taste of salt, he heaved.

"What are you–?!" Blaze began to protest, but broke off as she had the same realization. She ran to help him. Her muzzle fastened into the branch just beside his. They both heaved, the object creaking warningly, until finally there was a hearty crack, and it broke loose.

Sienna stumbled back, panting and stretching his jaw. "I thought we could–… I could… use it to float to shore."

"But that means…" Blaze looked out at the water.

"You can't do that! You'll sink and drown!" Scorch sputtered.

Sienna felt his stomach turn over.

"Besides," Flint said. "You're wounded."

"…I know."

"What if it doesn't work?" Blaze asked. It wasn't wholly a protest, but a simple question.

"Then I'll drown, and the Tribe will be lost at sea."

"And if it does?"

"Then I'll float to shore and find the Lutra village. I'll get us help. We'll be saved!"

Blaze's expression was unreadable.

"How about I go, instead? I've been up to my neck in water more times than I would have liked."

Sienna opened his mouth as though about to agree, then shook his head. "I wouldn't be able to live with myself if you didn't make it. It was my idea, I should be the one to do it."

Blaze grunted. Then, with a flick of her tail, she padded over to the other side of the raft.

"What are you…?" Sienna began.

Blaze's jaws fixed on a piece of driftwood, and a moment later, she moved back to him with a branch of her own, and dropped it beside his. "We can both go. How about that?"

Sienna stared at her with a mixture of horror and gratitude, before shaking his head. "N-no. But thank you."

"If you go alone, I'm following you. So we might as well agree to go together. Double the eyes, double the chance of finding the village, right?"

"If... if that's what it takes."

Sienna again looked out to the island of Indigna. It looked so far away, and the gap between them and the shore was growing. They had to go, and they had to go *now*.

Nausea rose in his gut as he watched the golden sunlight reflecting on the ocean's waves. The shore was close enough that he could have sprinted to it in moments on land. But just how long would it take to swim to?

...And who knows what swims beneath us.

Sienna shook his head, trying to shake off any reservations. The fur rose upright along his back and neck. He turned towards Blaze, then the other Ailura.

The others watched solemnly.

"Good luck, lad," Rusty breathed.

Sienna turned back towards Blaze.

"Ready?"

Blaze nodded. She picked up her driftwood branch in her muzzle, holding it tightly in sharp teeth. After a moment of hesitation, Sienna did the same. They exchanged one last look, and then turned to the shore. Sienna held his breath, closed his eyes, and jumped.

Freezing water closed around his head, filling his ears and chilling him to the bone. He floundered with his forepaws, fearing that the driftwood wasn't enough, and that he was sinking. But then he felt his nose breach the surface.

Sienna choked out water, gasping for air around the branch.

He bobbed, but didn't sink, forepaws flailing uselessly underwater.

A wave washed over his head. Sienna breathed in water and choked. He struggled, unable to pinpoint the direction he was facing.

His mind reeled, head spinning.

I have to open my eyes.

Fear tightened around his chest.

His eyes opened to a blurred haze of lights and

shadows. Was that the shore, or a trick of the sunlight on water? Was that the island or the raft?

It didn't matter. Full of terror, Sienna struck out towards a pale smear in his vision. His floundering paws sent up sprays of droplets. His back legs kicked him forward, and his tail dragged in the current.

He might have been swimming for minutes, or hours.

Either way, it was long enough for his clenched jaw to ache.

Finally Sienna felt his hindpaws sink into something soft. He wanted to cry out with relief, but was terrified of letting go of the driftwood.

Sienna kicked off it, powering himself forward. Soon he could stand again. He waded ashore, quaking, hacking and coughing. He felt heavier than he had ever felt before as he stumbled onto sand, the sea lapping placidly around his ankles. He finally unhooked his teeth from the branch.

Once he was clear of the water, Sienna sank down onto his side, heaving ragged breaths.

A sodden weight hit the sand next to him.

Chapter 4

Indigna

As his breaths evened out and the adrenaline subsided, Sienna became aware of the rising ache in his chest.

As he tried to ease himself to his paws, the pain spread like a sudden wildfire, and with every breath he felt his injured ribs sharply protest. He sank back down into the sand with a groan.

He closed his eyes, folded back his ears, and tried to even his breaths. They tasted like fish.

Flexing his forepaws, he felt the soft sand between his toes, and revelled in the sensation. It helped, even as the grains clung to his fur.

"Sienna…? Are you alright?"

A voice broke through the haze, muffled through what he presumed was water in his ears.

A moment later, Sienna cracked open his eyes. A blurred silhouette stood over him. In his panic, he had almost forgotten that Blaze had made the journey alongside him. She was already standing, though, her belly and chest white with a layer of sand.

"Yes, I'm… just catching my breath," Sienna answered.

"Well... you might want to hold it just a little longer," Blaze said, with gentle humour.

"Why's that?" Sienna asked.

"Look," Blaze said.

With no small amount of effort, Sienna raised his head, lifting himself onto his elbows, and then all four paws. He winced at his body's final protest, but didn't fall back down. Blaze stepped aside, and he looked past her.

She was right.

Beyond the sloped shore and its pristine white sands, Sienna had never seen anything so green.

Broad leaves trailed onto the sands, hanging from the gnarled branches of stout trees. As though in a trance, Sienna walked towards the treeline, and stood within their shadows, where he could see the wonders of the rainforest through golden pillars of light.

He struggled to peer over the blanket of narrow-leaved ferns that covered the ground, which rose as high as his head.

Colourful flowers peeked out from veils of shimmering leaves. Coils of ivy clung to tree trunks, hanging heavy with clusters of blue flowers and fruit that Sienna quickly recognized as bubbleberries. His mouth watering, Sienna took a few steps towards them.

His paws sank into a soft carpet of flowering moss. More confidently now, he strode a little further forward.

"At least we know where to find... whoa."

A fern curled away from Sienna as he brushed against it. Its narrow leaves coiled into one another until they were furled in a tight ball around the cluster of orange berries in its centre.

Sienna watched in amazement until the plant ceased to move.

If all of them did that, it would be far easier to clear a path. He exchanged a glance with Blaze, before taking an experimental step forward. The ferns withdrew from their touch, allowing Sienna and Blaze to press forward.

Small creatures, exposed by the sudden loss of cover, scurried away from them. What looked at first to be a patch of moss croaked, and sprang away as Sienna threatened to step on it.

As they reached the vine-covered tree, Sienna and Blaze looked up towards the shapes of the bubbleberries, hanging among broad, emerald leaves.

Small, golden creatures flitted through the air, poking their narrow heads into the flowers. They lingered just long enough for the Ailura to look at them; sometimes fluttering for an instant above their heads.

With whirring wings they hovered, serpentine bodies curling and whisking on the slightest breeze, a small tongue flicking in and out of a small, pointed beak. Tiny heads cocked and feathered crests fanned, they looked at the strange new creatures that had invaded their home.

As soon as Sienna turned to look at them, the creatures took flight, disappearing as though they were never there.

Even the long-dead husks of tree trunks wore elegant drapes of mosses and vines.

In the spaces where the trees ceased to grow, Sienna could see the twisted trunks of titanic mushrooms. Their broad caps trailed curtains of lichens and vines.

Even so close to the edge of the forest, Sienna couldn't help feeling overwhelmed. There were so many colours and lights and plants, the likes of which he had never before seen or heard of.

How could they possibly learn what was safe for them to eat?

What else lurked further in these woods?

And, most importantly, how could they possibly find the Lutra in a place like this?

"We should follow the river," Sienna decided, finally. "Remember what Indigo said? 'The village sits in a curve of the river's mouth'... so, that'll probably be easiest."

After a moment of thought, Blaze nodded, glancing up at the fruit above them. "Do you think we should stop to eat first?"

"I..." Sienna felt his stomach growl. He opened his mouth, momentarily about to agree.

But first, he looked back the way they had come.

Through the newly-cleared path of ferns he could see the ocean lit up gold by the evening sun. He struggled to make out the distant shapes of the Ailura, floating further and further away. "Let's... come back for food. When we find the Lutra." He hesitated. "What do you think?"

Blaze nodded, although she glanced longingly up at the fruit for a moment.

"Lead the way," she said finally.

"Ah, uh– are you sure?"

Blaze offered him an odd look. She gave his shoulder a bump with hers. "It was your idea to jump off the boat."

With a small nod, Sienna pressed on, feeling his friend following closely on his tail. When he turned back, one last time, he saw the ferns unfurling one by one to cover their trail. The ocean disappeared from sight.

Indigo slept like a rock, awakening only once, and only briefly, as he smelled the rich perfume of freshly-caught flitfish. He awoke to find them assembled in a neat pile by the entrance to his chamber. His stomach growling more than it had in years, Indigo devoured every single one of them, lay back down, and went back to sleep.

Time passed by unnoticed, unimportant.

He dreamt of swimming free through wide open seas, chasing colourful fish across bright coral reefs and watching the sun shine over shimmering underwater vistas.

Blissful life as he knew it played before his very eyes, excitement surging in his chest.

But above the sound of the waves, a voice called his name, familiar, and worried.

"Indigo...? Indigo, are you in there?"

The beautiful sights of submarine wonders faded into a dark abyss. Consciousness came spinning back as the blanket of slumber was tugged out of his grasp.

"Mhmm? Dad?" Indigo cracked open his eyes. "Yeah,

I'm in here. What's up?"

Tide's ocean-blue form pushed his way through the curtain of lichen. He looked Indigo over thoroughly before seeming satisfied.

Indigo pushed himself into an upright position, settling back on his haunches.

Tide glanced away for a moment. "I was... well, I was just worried about you."

Indigo blinked slowly. "Why worry?"

"It's been more than a full day. Not even food could rouse you for long. I thought perhaps you were hurt, or..."

Tide trailed off.

Indigo felt impatience tugging at the end of his tail. No matter what happened, Tide feared for him. And every single time, things turned out okay.

"I'm fine, see? What did Pa say?"

"Shimmer said that you'd be fine. But I wanted to come and ask you myself, just to be sure."

"Well, are you sure now?"

Tide hesitated, then nodded.

Indigo let out a breath.

"Good."

He didn't know how Shimmer dealt with his partner's worrying, sometimes. Reassurance proved futile, and the fear itself was unfounded and unnecessary. Even Tide knew that, so Indigo didn't need to tell him.

Besides, he heard enough of that from the other Lutra. Within a community where Lutra were expected to make a show of their true colours, Tide's reticence was strange. Scandalous, even, considering he was supposed to be a Queen.

"Will you be going back to sleep again?" Tide asked after a while.

Indigo blinked. Whilst grogginess still clung to his limbs and sleep clung to his eyes, Indigo didn't think he'd be going back to sleep. Especially if...

"Wait, how long did you say I'd been asleep?" Indigo asked, suddenly wide awake.

"Since yesterday," Tide repeated. "The sun is setting."

Indigo's fur prickled with discomfort. "The Ailura will be arriving soon. I promised Pa I'd go and check on them."

"You should wait until morning. It's dangerous to be out at night."

Indigo nodded. It would be fine. Surely it would be. Even if he'd broken another promise, all would be well. The Ailura weren't due to arrive until *tomorrow*. Even still, his fur prickled with unease, and a cold stone of dread was rapidly growing in his belly.

"I suppose they'll be fine."

Tide nodded.

"That being said, I... I need to go get some water. My throat feels like I ate sand."

Whiskers twitching with amusement, Tide nodded. "I'll let Shimmer know you're well."

"You do that."

Tide turned to leave, pulling the hanging moss aside with his tail to allow Indigo to pass through as well. With comfortable familiarity, they began to go their separate ways, when Tide stopped, and glanced back at him.

He opened his mouth, then closed it again, before nervously looking away.

"Oh, and... I'm sorry."

"Hm?"

"Just for... well... you know." Tide trailed off.

Indigo felt guilt clench in his belly, remembering the thoughts that had crossed his mind.

Tide knew about Indigo's misgivings.

Of course he knew.

He was Indigo's father; being anxious for his safety, no matter how much, was just a part of that.

As a child, he remembered the days when Tide would rather curl up alone than play in the ocean, which had always been a source of frustration. Tide's idea of spending time with his son had been weaving elaborate jewellery, something that the young Indigo had never found particularly entertaining.

The only things that had come out of Indigo's protests were murmured reminders from Shimmer that his father was always, always, trying his best.

Every year, Tide promised he would try to give the festival a go. Every year, he promised he would do better.

But he never did.

"It's fine," Indigo said, after a pause. "Sleep well."

Finding nothing more to say, they went their separate ways. On the water-powered lift, Indigo was gently lowered down to the waterfall pool, where he drank his fill.

And then, he set off through the village. But, rather than returning, he found his paws carrying him to the edge of town. He disappeared into the water and resurfaced to the cool evening air, and the sounds of the night creatures crying out.

Night soon fell, plunging the rainforest into darkness. Sienna and Blaze moved close together, unnerved by the chorus of calls and the sounds of things moving just beyond their sight. In the absence of sunlight, many of the flowers began to glow and broad leaves revealed the shining patterns of their veins.

Despite walking through a world of fluorescence, the Ailura found it near-impossible to navigate. Where life didn't glisten, the darkness was near-abyssal.

Even the sound of running water had faded into obscurity some time ago, and now they struck out blindly.

Sienna's ears stood upright, his fur prickling with fear. Each time something brushed against his pelt he'd startle, flinching back, and every time there was a hoot or a howl or a scream in the distance he would freeze until the sound had faded into distant echoes.

Finally Blaze moved to stand beside him, almost invisible in the dark. Her eyes glittered red in what little could be reflected.

"We should go back the way we came. Find the river again, and stick closer this time."

"Ah, uh, yeah. Good idea."

"Want me to take the lead?"

Sienna's skin flushed hot beneath his fur. "Do you... *want* to take the lead?"

Sienna didn't know why, but the thought of it made his heart sink, his stomach turning with embarrassment and a crushing sense of failure. This had been his idea, his chance, and he had led them into the middle of nowhere.

And it wasn't just Blaze relying on this; the other Ailura were somewhere out there, every single one of their lives hingeing on their success.

"Sure. I can do. I've seen much more of the way back than the way ahead."

"Really?"

"Yeah, well, your tail-end isn't exactly easy to see through."

As Blaze turned around, she clipped his ear with the end of her tail.

Sienna's spirits lifted slightly. As she moved forward, re-treading the pawprints in the moss, he followed closely behind. He heard quiet rustles as the ferns once again withdrew from their path.

As the soft rush of the river returned, Blaze began to veer her course towards it.

The cover of trees began to thin, the undergrowth gradually becoming less dense. Finally, as Sienna looked past her, he saw the distant glitter of the moons on the water.

But it wasn't long before Blaze stopped dead in her tracks.

"What is it?" Sienna whispered, moving forward so that he could look over her shoulder.

"Shh," hissed Blaze.

Something moved in the dark. Green feathers reflecting tones of red and gold rustled gently, a forked tongue tasting at the air. Two large eyes, glowing intensely gold under the moons, snapped towards them. The feathered serpent rose up into a threatening arch, pointed beak parted as it let out a low and guttural growl.

Unlike the littler creatures that flitted through the air, this one had no wings, its beak long and hooked.

It wasn't a large creature, but Sienna was unnerved.

We'll have to try and go around it, Sienna thought, nudging Blaze to try to get her attention. He watched her closely to see if she understood.

She nodded.

With cautious motions, they began to move around the creature.

It didn't like that.

The creature swayed as it watched them, its growls growing steadily louder. Unblinkingly, it stared.

Sienna stared right back, watching its every motion, his body taut with fear. He kept his full attention on it as he slid around.

Then he felt something crack beneath his paw. Sienna looked down to see a tiny pile of bones. The sound they made wasn't loud. It wasn't frightening. It wasn't even threatening.

But the creature's growl rose into a piercing screech. It rose up and puffed out the feathers along its neck and back. Before their eyes it swelled, puffing itself up many times its former size, and suddenly it was no longer a small serpent but a bristling, screaming monster, the iridescent tips of its feathers flashing hypnotically in the moonlight.

His ears still ringing from its scream, Sienna stared, afraid and hypnotized.

When it opened its beak he could see into the back of its throat. Despite Sienna's expectations, though, it didn't strike. It held its jaws firmly open and instead, spat.

And then he heard a guttural snarl. His vision was blotted out by a dark shape, knocking him out of his trance. Blaze stood before him, her still-damp fur puffed out, her tail twitching.

As he watched, she rose up onto her hindpaws, toweringly tall.

In all of his years, he had never thought of Blaze as being particularly impressive... But, as she towered over him, he was suddenly faced with the realization that her muscles were tough from years of metalworking, her fur nigh impenetrable by heat or impact. Her claws were thick, her paws calloused and hard from exposure to fire.

"Go, run!" Blaze snapped, jolting him from his stupor. "Find the village!"

Sienna didn't hesitate. He fled along the riverbank, and behind him heard the sound of two creatures locking in a life or death tussle.

He only stopped when he collided headlong with someone sprinting the opposite way.

It took a few moments for Indigo to come back to his senses after the impact. His vision spun, his nose stinging.

"Hey, watch where you're...–" he trailed off as he saw a pair of amber eyes gazing back at him, flashing like fire in the dark.

"Indigo? Is... that you?"

The Lutra's anger drained, like water down a sinkhole. Instead relief rose in its place. "Sienna!"

The Ailura stood before him, sides heaving, fur fluffed out.

Relief soon faded into fresh waves of dread.

There had been two sets of tracks in the sand.

"Wait, where's the–"

A piercing, keening scream cut him off, coming from somewhere in the rainforest beyond them. Sienna recoiled, whipping around to look in the direction of the noise.

To Indigo, it was a familiar sound; pythos were common at night, their terrifying cries helping to startle prey and deter predators.

Being so loud, they were easily avoidable, but their

reputation was part of the reason that the Lutra were reluctant to leave the village at night.

Although Sienna didn't answer, Indigo could see the gradual fall in his expression and knew the answer.

His heart sank.

"Are you serious?"

An answering scream left the Lutra's ears ringing. This one was alien to the rainforest of Indigna. It was low, and hoarse, and growling, almost a roar.

"...Blaze!" Sienna whispered.

Oh no, Indigo thought. He knew what he needed to do, but it came with a sinking feeling. *Is it worth it?*

Indigo paused, twitching, hesitating, as he stared into the trees. *Definitely not.*

The pythos screamed again, a gasping sound that was quickly silenced.

Oh... she's winning.

Indigo turned towards Sienna.

"Wait here," he ordered, in as authoritative a voice as he could muster.

Indigo charged ahead, leaving the Ailura where he stood.

A moment later the Lutra burst out of the undergrowth into the thick of the two warring creatures. The pungent smell of burned fur made his eyes water.

The pythos' venom was doing its work.

The two creatures writhed and thrashed.

Blaze's dark shape was wrapped up in the pythos' iridescent coils, but she bit and clawed ferociously wherever she could reach.

Picking his moment, Indigo lunged. He seized its tail in his jaws and bit down until blood welled in his mouth. The serpentine creature's grip tightened, and Blaze choked.

Indigo chomped until he felt his sharp teeth driving into bone.

A moment later it slackened, hissing and squawking. The serpent's coils relaxed, its puffed-out body slithering in reverse. In a glittering wave, its feathers lay down flat against its body, and suddenly it was just a small and harmless-looking snake. It spat at them, one last time, before fleeing into the forest.

Blaze slumped down, panting, her tongue lolling out between pointed teeth. Her red eyes were wide, and, luckily, unharmed. But the pythos' venom hissed and smoked as it ate away at patches of fur on her belly and sides.

Indigo heard a rustle, as Sienna stepped from the undergrowth, and bounded over to his friend.

"Don't touch her," Indigo warned, as the Ailura leaned in close ready to nose at her burnt patches of fur.

Sienna flinched, turning towards him for a moment.

"If the venom gets on you, it'll burn you, as well. Pythos aren't things you want to mess with on a whim."

Sienna frowned, but bowed his head. "Thank you."

"What are you doing here?" Indigo went on. "And more than that... How did you get here...? I thought your kind couldn't swim."

"The rafts were... getting too close to shore, too soon," Blaze panted. "We used pieces of driftwood to swim the rest of the way. We were looking for you; we need the help of the Lutra. The other rafts are already floating away."

Indigo wasn't certain he believed what they were saying. Him, *wrong?* He couldn't be *wrong!* He'd swam the seas all his life! How could he have made a mistake? "How close are they to shore?"

"I... don't know. A couple of tree-lengths, at most."

"And you say they're already floating away?"

"Yes," Sienna said. "And we need the Lutra to bring them in while they're still in reach of the island."

Indigo groaned inwardly. The Lutra wouldn't be happy about being ordered to work, not at this time of night. Indigo didn't know if he wanted to be the one to tell them, either... But he supposed that the Ailura were his responsibility now.

"We should go back to the village. I'll rally the Lutra, while you see the healers."

Sienna nodded.

Indigo took them along the riverbank, away from the ocean and towards a fork where part of the river split off into a tiny stream. They followed the stream for a time before pushing their way through a covering of ferns into a mossy entranceway that tightened around them into a claustrophobic tunnel. They made their way underground in a tight spiral.

The only sound was the steady trickle of running water. They felt its chill washing around their paws.

Soon, the musty smell of earth was replaced by the pungent, sharp aroma of fish, which intensified as they descended deeper underground.

A distant roar grew in Sienna's ears. Finally, the pale glow of moonlight pierced the dark. He and Blaze emerged from the tunnel beside the plunge pool of a silver waterfall. He looked out over the village; ribbons of water and foaming rapids filtering down over the different levels and between mossy mounds decorated with flowers, seashells, and glimmering jewels.

There were not many Lutra awake at this time of night, but as Sienna and Blaze crept around the waterfall pool for a better view, those that were awake came over to look at them.

As word spread, more and more appeared.

It was overwhelming; Sienna and Blaze had little time to take in even the wonders of the village. Lutra soon crowded them, muttering and murmuring amongst themselves, or firing volley after volley of questions.

Sienna lost track of Indigo in the hubbub.

"Have you really never been out to sea?"

"What was the other island like? Which way was it?"

"How did you get fur so beautifully red? Are those white patches real?"

"Just wait until Shard sees you!"

As soon as one voice finished their tirade of questions,

another began. Sienna's head spun with voices, sounds and colours, all intermingling with the distant crash of the waterfall. The crowd followed them even as they were taken by an overly-enthusiastic healer to the rapids, where Blaze was instructed to wash off the Pythos' venom.

Where at first the crowding had only consisted of the few who were awake, suddenly there were more, as eyes peering out of nearby dens caught sight of them. Curious Lutra were soon hurrying to join them on the plateau beneath the waterfall pool.

"Everyone, everyone! Leave these poor creatures alone," sounded a voice over the hubbub of voices. "Give them some space; I must speak with them."

Sienna felt his heart sing with relief as the torrent of voices died down into hushed whispers, and the surge of bodies retreated. A single Lutra approached, crystal-strung garb gently chiming as she moved.

Lilac fur was gently speckled with blue, and the white shading under her muzzle and belly echoed Indigo's. Her eyes caused Sienna to instinctively relax; they were understanding, and kind.

By the stranger's side stood Indigo, his head raised proudly, and his whiskers twitching.

"I am Shimmer, Queen of the Lutra. And you are… Sienna and Blaze, yes?"

Sienna's eyes opened wide with amazement. After a moment he froze, uncertain of whether to grovel or bow. In the end, he dipped his head as low as he could. Blaze quickly followed suit.

She knows our names!

"Oh, er, that's right! Yes, Miss Shimmer – er – sorry, your Majesty."

Shimmer's whiskers twitched with amusement. "Not a Miss, and… there'll be no need for that." Shimmer waved a paw to silence Sienna's sputtered apology. "Now, my son tells me that your kin floats on tiny islands, yes?"

"Your…?" Sienna exchanged a glance with Indigo, who grinned smugly back at him. Finally he looked at Blaze, now clean except for a few unfortunate patches of missing fur. She seemed just as surprised as he was.

Indigo is a... a prince?

He nodded. "Y-yes, that's right. We were driven away from our home island when the mountain started spewing fire."

A soft murmur rippled over the assembled crowds. Gasps and hushed noises of disbelief met Sienna's ears.

The lilac creature nodded. He cast his gaze around towards the other Lutra. "Indigo spoke of the same mountain, remember? They speak the truth."

Indigo raised his own voice. "I saw it for myself. The sky was black as if in a storm, but instead ash rained down from the sky."

Sienna shivered, as though a cold breeze had washed over him. He remembered it all too well. The disbelieving mutters soon died down into a loaded silence as realization set in.

"Blaze and I managed to get to shore, but the others can't swim. They're stuck out there, close to the island, but not close enough. We... need help."

More murmurs, soft whispers over whether it could possibly wait until morning.

"...And quickly."

A snowy white Lutra slid out of the crowd to stand by Shimmer's side. And although her expression was unreadable, Sienna did not much like the look in her one good eye.

"Nonsense," the white Lutra said. "It'll wait. Go eat, rest, and tend your newborns. All are far more important than these strange creatures."

"Shard–" Shimmer began, warningly.

"No, wait!" Sienna called out, fear showing in his voice. "Please, if we don't bring them to the island now, they could be lost forever!"

The gathered Lutra paused, stock-still and deadly silent, waiting for the word of their Queen.

"You will aid the Ailura. All who are healthy, uninjured, and strong enough to swim should go. That's an order."

Shimmer sent a scathing glance towards Shard who returned a long, and icy stare.

"Indigo?" the Queen went on. "Will you show them the way?"

Indigo cast a pointed look at Shard before bowing his head towards Shimmer. "Of course, father," he said, before breaking into a loping run. Indigo followed a winding path through the village, and the Ailura watched him go until he had disappeared into the dark.

One by one, the rest of the Lutra began to leave too, following Indigo across the village. Soon only the young, the old, and the snowy form of Shard remained.

"Fool," Sienna heard her mutter softly, as she turned away.

Shimmer paid her no heed.

Finally he turned towards Sienna and Blaze. "I hope you will forgive the lack of preparation. Indigo said that you liked the bubbleberries, but will you eat fish?"

Sienna's stomach ached with hunger, but the smell of fish didn't make him particularly excited to try it. Even so, he glanced sideways at Blaze. She must be starving after the long walk and her tussle with the pythos.

"I'm... not sure. We can give it a try. We usually just ate the plants that we grew ourselves on Veramilia," she said.

Sienna nodded, feeling his stomach growl. "Before the disaster, we had as little to do with the water as possible," he added.

"I see. I'll see what I can do. You're welcome to stay in the village until we have news of your kind. There are some empty dens by the eastern rapids, if the rabble grows too much."

"Thank you, your maj–"

"Please, Queen Shimmer will do," Shimmer said, with a whiskery smile.

"Thank you, Queen Shimmer."

Despite the moistness of the empty dwelling and the roar of the waterfall, it was easy for Blaze and Sienna to sleep.

As promised, later on in the night Shimmer brought them fish to eat. Although they were terribly hungry and extremely grateful, the stench alone was nearly enough to destroy their appetite. And unfortunately, they tasted even worse than they smelled. Sienna and Blaze argued in hushed voices over who would be the one to get rid of them to remove the smell from their den. In the end, it was Sienna who ended up darting from the cover of their den to dump what remained in the rapids.

As they bobbed away, watching him with sad, dead eyes, Sienna felt as though his mother's disappointment in him had been reincarnated.

The feeling only lasted until one of them was picked up by a Lutra cub further down the rapids. As though the fish was a plaything, it paraded the dead fish around its peers. Sienna couldn't hear what the cub was saying, but one by one, the faces of the townsfolk turned to look up at him.

Ashamed, Sienna slunk back to the den, where Blaze waited for him, stifling fits of laughter.

A few hours after that, Indigo returned, waking them completely unapologetically despite the intrusion. Blinking back sleep and yawns, the two Ailura stumbled after him, to where Shimmer was waiting.

Suddenly tense, Blaze and Sienna stood eagerly to attention as they awaited news of their kin.

Shimmer gave Indigo a small nod, indicating that it was his turn to speak. His chest swelled with pride as he did so.

"The Ailura are safe. Every one of the floating islands has been safely brought to shore."

For the first time since leaving Veramilia, Sienna felt like laughing with pure relief and joy. Their village was safe. Their kind was alive, and they had finally got away from that accursed island!

"...However, they're refusing to enter the village. The thought of being near so much water scares them too much. They've set up camp in the clearing above us."

Indigo turned towards his father.

Shimmer nodded, slowly. "Good, well done."

"So... What will happen to us now?" Blaze asked.

"I've been thinking, speaking with Tide... and we think it would be best if you go your own way. Try to find somewhere that you can set up a village to your own tastes. You mentioned living on a mountain, yes?"

Sienna and Blaze nodded.

"Well, the Red Mountain sits further into the mainland of Indigna. The forest there isn't quite so thick, and there are plenty of caves and some ruins there which you might use."

"Ruins?"

"From a time long gone. They are irrelevant to us. Anyhow... since you're inexperienced when it comes to living on Indigna, you'll need a guide." Shimmer turned towards his son, who blinked back with confusion written in his whiskers. "And... since Indigo has been the one to find you, feed you, and organize your rescue, he will be the one to take you up the mountain, as well."

Sienna turned towards Blaze. Her eyes sparkled, tail twitching with nerves. He was certain that he looked much the same.

"You're free to leave whenever you're ready."

The Queen dipped his head, and turned away from them.

Sienna glanced over at Indigo. To his surprise, though, the Lutra said nothing, looking after Queen Shimmer with his mouth slightly open.

Noticing Sienna's glance, Indigo turned towards him, awkwardly clearing his throat. The Lutra forced a smile. "Er, gimme a second," he muttered. A moment later, Indigo had turned away from them and bounded after his father.

"Pa, wait!"

Indigo was already panting by the time he caught up with the Queen, both from the run, and from the shock of it all. "What was that for?"

"What do you mean, 'what was that for?'" Shimmer seemed amused.

"That! You know, the guide thing?"

"You've done a good job at taking care of the Ailura the past few days. Don't you want to continue?"

"Well, yes, but..." Indigo paused, lowering his voice. "Don't you think I deserve a day off?"

"Indigo... there are more important things to be concerned with than taking days off. We have a village to save. Not just one creature. A *village,* Indigo."

"Well, yes, but... I'm a *princess.* Don't you think I've done enough for the Ailura already?"

His father's disappointment was tangible.

"You know, Indigo. Being a Princess isn't about relaxing and avoiding responsibilities. You almost missed your chance to help the Ailura at all!"

Indigo winced. It was difficult to find a comeback for that one.

"As a Princess, and even more importantly, as an *adult*, you need to learn from things like this. Times are changing, and I have a feeling that we're going to need a good Queen."

"You *are* a good Queen."

"I won't always be."

"...We are *Lutra*. We'll *adapt*."

"Exactly. That means you too."

"Huh?"

"That means this is an order, Indigo. Go and guide the Ailura."

Indigo's heart sank.

"Now?"

He turned to see that Blaze and Sienna were waiting for him. They must have been eager to leave.

"Now."

Indigo bit his tongue to keep back a sharp retort. Lowering his head and quietly seething, he slunk over to the fluffy creatures.

"I'll see you soon, okay?" he heard his father call out after him. "Love you!"

Indigo didn't reply as he led Sienna and Blaze up the secret tunnel and onto the surface world, where dawn was slowly breaking with a cold shower of rain.

Chapter 5

The Journey

When Sienna pushed out of the hidden tunnel and into fresh air the first thing he did was hesitate, twisting his sensitive ears to the sounds of the forest. Although every muscle ached to burst out into the foliage and search for his kin, memories of last night's tussle rose to the forefront of his mind and held him back.

Blaze seemed equally wary, ears forward and her paws falling soft against the mossy ground as she moved to stand next to him.

But the blue form of Indigo rippled ahead of them without hesitating even for a moment. Despite the Lutra's comparative clumsiness on land, Sienna found himself encouraged by his confidence.

Afraid of being left behind, Sienna and Blaze soon followed side-by-side.

The distant sound of voices rose above the whispers of the early-morning breeze. As he heard them, Sienna's breath caught in his throat, and he sped up, trotting past Indigo and pushing ahead. The flowing tendrils of the ferns jerked back out of his way.

As he pushed through the last few fronds, he felt all eyes fix on him. All those who were awake glanced his way. From those who wandered carrying rocks or fruits, to a few who had presumably been placed as watchers, all fell silent in their hushed conversations.

Feeling tension rising in his belly, Sienna took the opportunity to look around him.

The Ailura Tribe had claimed a fairly barren clearing as their camp; there was no thick undergrowth to lose one another in, and the sheltering cap and foliage trailing from a towering mushroom seemed to be serving as a sleeping den for the wounded and old. Most of their numbers, though, lounged throughout the clearing. The Tribe had completely ravaged a bubbleberry vine hanging from a vast tree trunk at the western edge of the clearing: it was stripped of all fruits within reach. The remnants of the round, purplish fruits lay scattered around the clearing, with a few intact specimens arranged in a neat pile towards its centre.

Seeing this, Sienna's stomach began to growl again.

But before he could even consider taking one, a familiar voice called out.

"Miss Blaze, is that you?"

From the edge of the clearing, Scorch came bounding over. At the sound of his voice, a few of the sleeping Ailura awakened. The guards began to leave their posts, surprise etched on their faces.

"By the Fire!"

"You're okay! Both of you!"

Soon the Ailura that had been sleeping began to push themselves upright, as the Tribe's remaining number gathered around in a broad circle. Sienna swept his gaze over the crowd to see faces both familiar and new, their eyes shining with relief and joy.

"It's Caldera's lad! And the young blacksmith!"

"They're the ones that jumped off the rafts and into the ocean!"

"How did they possibly survive?"

"They didn't just survive! These two saved us all!"

Flint's slate-grey form pushed to the forefront, greeting Blaze with a small dip of his head.

"But… it's not over yet. We're on the island, but what now?" a familiar voice, hoarse with age, broke in.

Sienna's gaze fitted over the crowd before finally settling on Rusty. The blacksmith was sitting upright, having been awakened by the commotion. His half-tail flicked as he struggled to stand.

Flint opened his mouth as though to reply, but then turned towards Sienna.

After glancing at Blaze, who nodded, Sienna turned to face them. He answered for all the Ailura to hear, casting a glance around the crowd. "This Lutra – Indigo – is going to guide us up the mountain, to find a new home."

A whisper spread among the Ailura. A few gazes lingered on Indigo.

Finally, Rusty spoke up again. "So you're certain this…" Rusty paused. "Stranger… will help us?"

Sienna nodded. "He's brought us this far. We wouldn't have made it to the island if it weren't for him."

"Besides," Blaze added. "The Lutra know the island better than any of us."

A muffled murmur of approval. A few nodded, but Rusty didn't seem convinced.

"If he keeps his word… then, that's all well and good."

"I'm certain that he will," Sienna said, casting a long glance towards the Lutra.

"And if he doesn't?"

"…Right now, our concern should be on finding a home. And to do that, we need all the help we can get," Blaze spoke with an air of finality.

"He'll guide us, then. But… who will *lead* us?" He paused. "In a strange land, with strange creatures and… strange *natives*, we'll need one of our own to stand at our head, as well. Someone capable and strong. To keep us – and him – in line."

Murmurs of agreement passed over the crowd.

"But… who?" Flint asked.

A few volunteers stepped forward, all of them shrugged

off or ferociously debated. As the conversation heated, Sienna felt a few eyes boring into his fur.

Someone stepped forward, her eyes bright and posture certain. She spoke the words he knew everyone was secretly thinking. "I was thinking, perhaps Caldera could lead us. That bone-headed stubbornness could be just what we need. That will could break mountains."

Sienna felt his eyes blur, and his limbs grew heavy. He looked away, but knew that they were waiting for an answer.

"Her fire... has gone out," Sienna said eventually.

He heard a few sharp intakes of breath.

"But that means..." Rusty trailed off. "Her mantle would fall to the next in her line."

The eyes on Sienna intensified. For a moment, he wanted nothing more than to run and cry. Although he was his mother's son, he knew better than anyone that he was not the one to carry her flame. Where Caldera's will could have sent mountains crashing down, Sienna would rather climb to the top simply to admire the view. He was many things, but a leader was not one of them. Sienna felt the fur around his eyes grow damp as he blinked away the tears, but finally he let out a breath.

"Then... that would be Blaze."

Sienna lifted teary eyes to look to his best friend.

Her red eyes blinked back at him in stunned silence. "Sienna, I–"

"No, Blaze... I... I can't lead us to our new home. But you..." He turned now towards the assembled Ailura. "If Blaze hadn't rallied the blacksmiths to make the rafts, we never would have got away from Veramilia. If she hadn't evacuated the village, there wouldn't be nearly so many of us here now."

He blinked once more as his eyes blurred.

"When we were cubs, Caldera took Blaze in as one of her own, and raised us together. I was never any more than my mother's apprentice, but Blaze... she took on her father's forge and became a blacksmith all on her own. She's always forged her own path, and I'd trust her to do the same for us all." He paused for a moment. "…If she'd want to, that is?"

Blaze blinked in stunned amazement.

"I, er…" Blaze stumbled over her words. A moment later, she shook her head, and straightened up. "If you're sure, then…" Her expression hardened slightly. "I'll give it my best shot."

"Now, does anyone have any objections?"

The Blacksmiths came crowding around her first, touching noses and brushing sides. They led the rising clamour in support of their newly-elected chief.

"Congratulations, Miss Blaze!" sang Scorch.

"You'll do great." Flint said.

"Wait–" Rusty began, but was soon drowned out by raised voices clamouring in support of their newly-elected chief.

As Sienna caught a glimpse of his friend through the crowd, he saw that her eyes were lit up with a new fire.

After Indigo had finished watching the Ailuras' debate in a somewhat perplexed manner, it was finally time for him to take the lead. The plan was for him to guide the Ailura upstream, following the river further into the mainland.

Indigo was largely unfamiliar with this area; he was an ocean creature, and rarely set foot among the trees. So it was decided that he would head upstream first to plan their route and work out any potential dangers, before going back for the rest of the Tribe.

The new chief of the Ailura did, however, send a scout to travel alongside him. Their job was to learn the lay of the land, search for suitable places to call home, and take lessons from everything Indigo knew. Indigo also suspected, however, that they wanted to keep an eye on him.

His assigned companion turned out to be Sienna.

"Sienna was a farmer back home," Blaze had explained. *"He climbed the mountain every single day. He knows exactly what to look for when it comes to land, and he's good at navigating it, too!"*

Indigo was somewhat pleased; he had been expecting his companion to turn out to be miserable and crusty like Rusty, or quiet and stoic like Flint.

Sienna was neither of these, though like the rest of his kind, he was quite serious.

When they first set out, the Ailura was noticeably jittery, pausing every few paces to prick his ears and sniff the air. While Indigo tolerated it at first, he quickly grew impatient, and tired of waiting for him to catch up.

"What are you doing?" the Lutra asked, as Sienna paused once more.

"I'm listening out for danger," Sienna replied. "There's a lot moving in the woods."

Understandable, Indigo supposed. The Ailura were, after all, in a new land, full of new creatures and new hazards. But that was what he was there for. "Well, there's no need. We'll be fine."

"What about that thing we ran into last night? The angry ball of feathers that screamed?"

"What, the pythos? They only come out at night. You're perfectly safe out here during the day. Especially when you're with me."

"What about the squalls?"

"Sea-fliers. They don't venture inland."

"Aren't there any other predators?"

"Of course. But none stupid enough to pick a fight with a Lutra."

"If you say so."

Although Sienna didn't seem convinced, progress was noticeably quicker from that point on, much to Indigo's relief. They moved ahead in relative silence, with Indigo quickly running out of ideas on how to lighten the mood.

On the few occasions he tried to initiate a chase or playful wrestle, Sienna would simply look at him somewhat awkwardly, and then continue to walk in silence some time after.

For the first time since the Ailura's hectic rescue, though, Indigo had the chance to properly *look* at him.

Sienna moved ahead of Indigo with the curious lumbering motions typical of his kind. The Ailura were bizarre. They weren't graceful like the Lutra. They were rough-looking, heavy-set and reeked of smoke. The afternoon sunlight lit up his red-brown pelt in tones of fire, white markings standing out sharply against his fluffy face.

As his companion's striped tail waved out behind him, Indigo was hit with the near-uncontrollable urge to bite it.

"So, is it far?" Sienna asked sometime after noon, bringing Indigo out of his bored stupor.

Indigo glanced sideways at him, seashell necklace softly clacking. "Hmm?"

"Up the mountain, I mean."

"Oh, yes, well... That depends where you decide to call home in the end. It's about a week's walk to the mountain's peak, at least for a Lutra."

"Have you ever been there?"

"No. We rarely venture inland. I know only what the Riverfolk tell."

"Ah. I see."

The silence stretched on.

"So... what was it like, on the island?"

"It was... life. Not really much to it. We ate and slept and saved rations for the next day. There wasn't much to go around. Everyone had their place in making things work. I can't remember a day when I wasn't working on my mother's farm." Sienna paused. When he spoke again, there was an intensity in his tone that caught Indigo by surprise. "Blaze and I spent our lives thinking of how to leave that damned rock, when we had the chance."

For once in his life, Indigo was quite stuck on words to say. Lutra often left their village, swimming for greater seas or journeying inland with the Riverfolk. But their leaving was something to be celebrated, their memories of the village never sour. Usually, they would return each year for the festival with brand new stories to tell.

Indigo could hardly imagine growing up to hate the island of Indigna with such a burning passion.

"It... doesn't sound like you had much of a life back there."

"Well..." Sienna trailed off. Looking away, he moved ahead.

Indigo watched after him, but quickly lost interest and hurried to catch up. The small golden shapes of the flower-feeding plumaries darted overhead, heading for new foraging grounds on the other side of the river.

"What are those?" Sienna asked, his nose following one that flitted low across their path. "They seem to be everywhere."

"We call them gilded plumaries," Indigo said. "Lovely, aren't they?"

Sienna nodded, watching the little creature settle on a nearby plant with broad leaves and bright red flowers. Indigo perked up, and followed it.

"Oh, here's something you'll like!" he beamed.

When Sienna caught up, Indigo had stopped before the plant, which was teeming with the small creatures.

"You can use these little guys to see if a plant is poisonous, see? When the flowers turn into fruits, the plumaries can't eat them anymore, but you can!"

Sienna blinked. "So if a plant doesn't have any plumaries on it...?"

"Steer clear."

"I see," Sienna murmured, nudging at one of the leaves.

The plumaries hovering around the plant scattered, forming a great golden cloud as they took to the trees.

Sienna flinched back at the sudden movement, ears flattening against his head and fur bristling, whilst Indigo watched and giggled. As he straightened up again, the Ailura shook his head. "We should keep moving. We need to find our next camp before nightfall."

"Oh? Right. Sure."

They hurried on, and in time the trees by the river

grew sparser. It was at this point they moved under the cover of the canopy, looking for a space to stay that wasn't quite so exposed to the elements. Occasionally, though, Sienna would stop, motion to a plant, and turn to Indigo.

"What about this plant?" he'd ask. "Is this edible?"

Indigo's answers were just as varied as the plants themselves. He never gave just a yes or no; there was always a catch or footnote. Soon Sienna's head was spinning with new words and information.

"Those are called Scorch Fruits! Eat them if you must, but they taste like fire! You might like them!"

"Oh, yes! Eat one, eat one! You'll love them! –See?"

"Oh, no, not that one! That's a burberry- they taste sweet but they cling to *everything*! Do you want to spend the rest of your days picking it out of your teeth?"

"Yes, eat those! They're delicious, but not *too* many, or you'll begin to stumble!"

Sienna was only satisfied when he ran out of new fruits to point out.

They eventually found a clearing which would suit their purpose for the night, and they could still hear the distant rush of the water to keep them oriented.

Finally, Sienna and Indigo returned to the Tribe.

As the sun went down, they led the Ailura upriver on the first leg of their journey.

The next day, Sienna and Indigo scouted ahead once more. As the tree cover along the riverbank continued to thin out, so too did the wildlife they encountered. Luckily, other than an early morning shower, the weather was crisp and clear. In the distance they were even able to catch the first glimpse of their destination, the Red Mountain. Its jagged peak scraped the sky, and the rich forest on its foothills gradually tapered off towards its peak.

The distant glitter of the river, a thin line of silver zigzagging down its slope, caught Sienna's eye. His fur tingled with excitement.

Surely with trees and water, it would be easy to find their new home?

With renewed enthusiasm, Sienna hurried on, hearing Indigo panting behind him as he struggled to keep up. Sienna turned to wait for him, watching Indigo approach with amber eyes sparkling. The Lutra were a strange race, with their long bodies and short legs. They certainly weren't made for journeys like this.

Their bodies, their gills, their webbed paws. Even the vast array of colours they came in: all were perfectly suited to the water.

Sienna recalled seeing Indigo floating in the waves from the raft, perfectly in his element.

"Would you like to rest?" Sienna asked, as Indigo came to a halt, sides heaving.

"What, me? Of course not," Indigo huffed, shaking his head. "It's not even noon."

The Lutra turned his attention to the path ahead. The land was beginning to slope, the river dropping away from them and into a shallow ravine.

Sienna saw him glance longingly down at the river for a moment.

The Ailura took a moment to peer at the world around them. He suspected that Indigo was acting out of pride, so if he needed to rest, the best way to accomplish that would be to distract him.

Sienna's attention was drawn to a nearby plant, its leaves messy with coils bearing clusters of fruit that were small, round, and white.

There seemed to be no creatures around to feed on it, and so, he approached it.

As he did so, Sienna noticed that the plant's green roots were plainly visible against the surface of the earth, their tips tickling Sienna's fur as he drew near.

Its sugary smell reached out to him. His nose twitched to it, but, remembering Indigo's words, he hesitated. The

Plumaries left this plant alone, which, if Indigo was to be believed, then–

"*Wait!* Stay away from that!"

The sheer panic in Indigo's tone surprised him.

Sienna backpedalled, jumping backwards and away from the plant. He looked to Indigo expectantly.

"See those fruits?" Indigo nodded at the small, white clusters. "We call those death pearls."

Sienna felt a shiver passing through his fur. "Are they poisonous?"

"If you eat a death pearl, your limbs will go stiff and you won't be able to move. Then the plant's roots will wrap around you and slowly drain you."

Sienna shivered, his fur raising.

"That's awful."

"True, but it can have its uses. The healers in our village use death pearls to numb pain and keep wounds clean."

"Does Blaze know about these?"

"Yes, yes, I warned her. Though, they're quite rare."

"Even still. It's something to think about when choosing a home. Can they be destroyed?"

"Destroyed?" Indigo seemed confused by the idea. "I... don't know. We've never tried."

"How do you keep your village safe from it, then?"

"We teach about it."

"Is that enough?"

"Well... we do have the occasional tragedy, but it's usually the healers and apprentices who don't harvest the berries properly. I don't see any need to destroy them; especially when they keep so many other things alive!"

"They do? How?"

"Some special herbs and flowers only grow beneath their tendrils, and some creatures can eat them too. And, when the death pearls fall into the river, whatever eats them makes easy prey for us. And that's all without even considering their medicinal uses."

"I see," Sienna murmured, thinking it over. When Indigo described it like that, it made a lot of sense, but

Sienna still wasn't keen on the idea of allowing them to thrive so close to his kin.

"I still want to make sure there's nothing like this nearby when we set up our next camp," he decided. "We have young, and the death pearls smell delicious."

"Of course, of course!"

Energy seemingly restored, Indigo trotted around him and pranced ahead, his clumsy gambolling making Sienna smile despite himself.

"Shall we go on?" Indigo asked.

"Of course."

Breaking into a brisk trot, Sienna followed along behind.

By early afternoon, it began to rain once more, a gentle shower of tiny droplets that soaked Sienna to the bone and left him shivering. Eager to take shelter, he and Indigo branched away from the river and huddled together under the cap of a vast mushroom.

The rain showed no sign of stopping but when Sienna felt suitably dry, they slunk out from their shelter, deciding to remain beneath the tree canopy. Here, they spent some time looking for a suitable area to make camp. After searching until early evening, they finally stumbled upon an area of the woods bare of growth and moss, where ancient stones stood in worn formations.

While some of the structures were intact enough to still be considered walls, most were no more than piles of rubble by now.

Sienna traced the foundations of the structures, moving in a slow circle around the well-worn stones. "They look like... no... that's impossible," Sienna muttered, as he paced around the clearing. He raised his head and scented the air, but nothing remained. The only sound that reached his ears was the pitter-patter of the rain on the tree canopy.

"What is it?"

"They look like the old buildings on the edge of the village... The Ailura Village... but that wouldn't make sense."

"Back on Veramilia?"

"Yes."

"Are you certain?"

"I…" Sienna paused. "I'm not sure."

Still, they rang with familiarity, the shapes echoed the dome-like structures that had been the homes of the ancient Ailura. The homes that they'd recently left behind.

Sienna paced about the clearing, inspecting what might have been dens, once. The world around them began to grow dark, even as Sienna continued his fervent explorations. They would have to leave soon, and they still hadn't found a place to make camp. But… the longer Sienna thought about it, the more certain he was.

"We'll bring the Tribe here for the night," Sienna said to Indigo. The Lutra looked up at him in surprise. The clearing wouldn't suit them forever, but it would do for one night. The walls that still stood would make nice shelter, provided the rain wasn't too heavy.

The nearby trees bore fruit, and with the river a distant rumble, they would have everything they needed here.

Besides…

"I want to bring Blaze here. She spent her life studying the ancients' work. She'll know."

Indigo cast a long look around. "…Are you sure?"

Sienna hesitated, then nodded.

"Alright then. Let's head back."

The rest of the Ailura arrived that night, some time after the sun had set. There was a myriad of mutterings and excited gasps as the settlers made their way into the clearing, and were greeted with the familiar traces of home.

Soon, the guards were taking their places. Exhaustion was already setting in. By the time the last of the travellers arrived, the first were already sleeping within the crumbled walls or in the open, in warm piles.

Indigo left to go and swim in the nearby river, claiming that his paws felt too dry from all the walking.

Once the Tribe was settled, Sienna went straight to Blaze; they settled together at the edge of the clearing, talking in low voices.

"So, what do you make of these ruins, then?"

"This is... not a lot to go on, but... these ruins bear a striking resemblance to those of the Ancient Ailura. I can tell you that much."

"So... these walls...?"

"Yes?"

"How can you tell?"

"The structure, more than anything. From the marks in the stone I can see how they were carved... and it's the same as on the island. Even some traces of clay here and there. The architectural style, too... it feels familiar, don't you think?"

Sienna nodded. "Anything else?"

"These are far older than the ruins on the island. But... if they are ancient Ailura ruins, that's a given, I suppose."

"What do you mean?"

"Do you remember the legend? We weren't always from Veramilia. Our kind had to have come from somewhere. And... perhaps this is where."

Of course Sienna remembered the legend. But... when he thought back to the reaction of the Lutra when they had entered the village for the first time, something didn't sit right. Their amazement and profound awe. None of them had seemed to recognize their kind even for a moment, not even from legend. Could they really have originated here?

"But then..." Sienna hesitated. He lowered his voice even further, leaning in to speak almost directly into her ear. "The legends also speak of monsters that drove us from our home. Monsters that wanted to put an end to our ancient ways."

"That's..." Blaze glanced around. "That's what I'm worried about, too."

"What will we do?"

"I'm… not sure. With any luck, the monsters are long gone."

"And if they're not?"

"Well then, we'll just have to figure something out."

"If you say so. But this place… it's…"

"Perfect?" Blaze smiled lightly.

"Yes. In all of my wildest dreams, I could never have imagined a place like this."

Blaze nodded. "Me too. It's almost too good to be true."

"…Yeah."

Sienna looked up towards the sky, towards where the light of the Mothering Moon shone faintly through the leaves. He fell silent for a time, staring upwards, as the trees rustled in a gentle evening breeze.

"We should probably get some sleep," Sienna said finally.

Blaze looked at him, her red eyes shimmering in the dark. "We should," she chuckled. "You especially. How's your wound healing?"

"It aches, but it's fine."

"Good. Be sure not to strain yourself too much tomorrow, okay?"

Sienna blinked, offering a lopsided smirk. "If you say so, Chief."

Blaze gave his snout a playful swat with her paw, leaving Sienna with a stinging nose and a grin on his face.

"Good work, today," Blaze said, just as Sienna began to leave. "I'm sure we'll figure it out. We have the Lutra helping us, after all."

Sienna nodded.

"We've lasted this long."

Blaze chuckled. "By some miracle."

Sienna smiled. "Burn Bright."

Blaze nodded back at him. "Burn Bright."

And with that, they parted ways. Sienna picked out a ruin at the very edge of the clearing, and curled up in its shadow. Alone, ears tilted to the singing of the rainforest and the whispers of the breeze, he fell into a deep and peaceful slumber.

In the following days, the mountain loomed nearer and larger.

Indigo and Sienna found more clusters of ruins which they lingered around, sniffing and exploring. Indigo personally didn't see what made them so special, but he let the Ailura have his fun.

"What are you doing?" Indigo asked finally, as they stopped at one more crumbled ruin. The Lutra waited nearby, the end of his tail flicking with impatience, as Sienna sniffed around the old stones. There was nothing around here for him to do. No creatures for him to chase, or berries to play with.

This cluster of ruins was strange, however; even Indigo could admit that. One building in particular had withstood the test of time. It was a tall, pillar-like structure with a small entrance at its base. Indigo couldn't work out what it might have been used for. Despite his curiosity, he found himself reluctant to enter and instead nosed around the entranceway with bristling whiskers.

Sienna lifted his head from where he nosed at a flaky patch of rust. "I'm seeing if there's anything here that can be salvaged," he explained.

"Why?" Indigo asked.

"These are ancient Ailura ruins," Sienna said. "Or at least, we think they are."

"Really?"

"Well, they look just like the ones back on Veramilia. And this one here?" Sienna nodded up towards the hollow pillar. "This one proves it."

"Oh?" Indigo's voice trailed off. His attention followed a plumary as it flitted overhead, and lit on a nearby bubbleberry vine.

Sienna didn't appear to notice his companion's lapse in attention. He moved towards the pillar, slowly circling it.

"Yes, well. This one used to be a forge. It's where we make metal and tools. The ancients perfected the skill to an extent that hasn't been mastered since. On Veramilia, there was very little metal to be found."

"I thought this was the first time you'd come to Indigna?" Indigo reminded him, with a curious twitch of his whiskers.

"It is. But legends say we didn't always live on Veramilia."

Indigo found it difficult to imagine that his kind would forget the existence of an entire race. And something niggled at him like a flea on his back that he couldn't quite reach.

But then again… *had* they forgotten?

It was rare that the Lutra ventured inland, and rare that the Ailura ventured close to water. Perhaps the ancient Ailura and Lutra had never met at all.

Curiosity and frustration growing within him simultaneously, Indigo shrugged off the thought. There was no point in dwelling on something they could never know.

"Why would you want to salvage anything? Indigna has everything you need without pulling junk out of long-dead ruins."

"Well, I…" Sienna's white-pointed brows furrowed. "We could make use of them. If any metal remains we can recycle it into tools."

"Do you really need them?"

"They make things far easier when it comes to farming the land and defending ourselves. But I…" Sienna hesitated. "I suppose we don't need them right now."

"Right! Maybe when you find a new place to build your village. And then you can show me what all the fuss is about."

To Indigo's relief, Sienna nodded. "…Besides," he said. "It would be silly wasting our strength carrying useless metal up the mountain, when we've got so far to go."

"Yes, yes!" Feeling that they'd drawn the conversation to a close, Indigo motioned to the nearby vine bearing bubbleberries. "Do you want to stop for something to eat before we keep going?"

"You, too?"

Indigo opened his mouth, then closed it again. As much as the Ailura seemed to enjoy the fruits, Indigo did not much like them. In his eyes, all they were good for was watersports. "I think I'll wait and see if the river comes up to meet us," he said after a while. "I prefer to hunt for my food."

Sienna's whiskers twitched. "Perhaps we should bring some along with us, then," he mused. "In case you can't find anything."

"Only if you carry it!"

Sienna let out a small snort, before moving over to the vine. He soon ate his fill.

When he had finished, Indigo waited until Sienna had selected the best-looking fruit to bring along with them, and then they continued at a steady trot.

As Indigo had hoped, the river soon began to climb higher up the ravine in a series of small waterfalls and rapids. Soon, the ravine became a shallow riverbank, and shortly after that they came to a small lake where the mountain stream collected.

At this sight, Indigo let out a small, gleeful chirp, drawing Sienna's curious gaze. Before the Ailura could move to stop him, Indigo had darted forward and plunged into the clear water.

It was colder than Indigo was expecting and not very deep, but having not swam in days, Indigo was overjoyed. He felt the water ease the dirt from his claws and soothe the dust from his gills.

He chased small creatures for a time beneath the surface, none of them big enough to fill his belly, before realizing that Sienna was probably waiting for him.

Peering through the silver veil of the surface and towards the bank, Indigo felt his spirits lift. The Ailura was pacing, looking for him, and yet never seeing. His mouth opened up in a silent call, having left the fruit away from the water's edge.

Indigo's whiskers wiggled, a thrill of mischief running down his spine. His gills flared with the faintest laugh as he paddled quietly nearer to shore, leaving barely a ripple on the surface above him.

Sienna overlooked him. His amber eyes glanced about wildly, ears pricked. Indigo hugged the bottom of the lake, sediment swirling around him.

Indigo burst up above the surface.

He blew out through his nose, spraying Sienna with a jet of water, before darting back below. The Lutra resurfaced not far from the bank. Suddenly soaked, Sienna blinked at him with a mixture of shock and confusion, fur standing on end.

Indigo grinned, floating just a bit away from the bank.

"What was that for?!" Sienna asked. As he caught sight of Indigo's smirk, the stunned expression gradually faded from his face. "Oh... right."

Indigo giggled.

Sienna still didn't laugh, wearing a mock scowl. As the Lutra paddled nearer, he reached a paw into the water and kicked up a splash. It didn't hit.

"I'll get you back for that," Sienna grumbled, shaking himself off. Indigo was amused to see that it didn't help any.

Indigo narrowed his eyes, floated a little nearer, and then, as Sienna stooped to pick up the bubbleberry, did it again.

This time Sienna wasn't quite so surprised.

"Stop that!" he said, although Indigo didn't think he meant it.

He sent another splash Indigo's way, droplets sliding harmlessly off of the Lutra's fur.

Indigo, in response, turned onto his back, using his powerful tail to kick up a huge splash. When the water had calmed, Sienna stood on the shore soaked to the bone, sending Indigo into peals of laughter.

Sienna glared at him. But, drippy and droopy, he didn't look very threatening.

"Hey! Pass me the bubbleberry!" Indigo said suddenly.

"What, why?"

"You'll see, just pass me it!"

The Ailura took the purple fruit into his mouth and dropped it into the water. It disappeared for a moment, and then bobbed to the surface near the Lutra. Indigo placed a testing paw upon it, pushing it down, only for it to bounce back up. When he nudged it, it floated away.

After a moment of batting at it with his paws, Indigo hit it with his tail sending it skimming across the surface over to Sienna, where it bounced ashore.

"Now send me it back!"

"Why?"

"Just do it!"

Sienna hit the bubbleberry with one of his forepaws, and sent it bouncing back across the water towards Indigo.

Indigo swam towards it, pulling it under the water, and bouncing it back up. A moment later he sent it to Sienna once again, who nudged it back without needing to be told.

"That's it!" encouraged Indigo, using a powerful kick to launch himself out of the water and send it back.

Since he was soaked already, Sienna waded into the water to catch it. He smacked it back to Indigo before it came to a full stop.

This time Indigo headbutted it back across the water.

Sienna missed; wading up to his chest to retrieve it before continuing.

Indigo sent it back with a powerful stroke of his tail.

Sienna didn't miss the next time.

The two companions played until the sun dipped low in the sky, and they were both panting as they finally hauled themselves ashore.

"I'm gonna be feeling this tomorrow," Sienna said with a groan. "I can't believe you managed to rope me into this for so long."

Indigo snorted, and grinned.

"I can't believe it took so long for *you* to figure it out."

"Well, I've never done anything like it before."

"I figured. I think it's the first time I've seen you smile."

In response, Sienna did smile. "It's been a while since I've had a reason to."

"Oh, come on. There's plenty! There's so much to smile about. You survived, for one, and now you can all live on the island of Indigna with us! There's no better place than this."

"I suppose there isn't."

He looked up. "Speaking of, we should try and find a place to set up camp. Do you think the lake shore will do?"

Indigo looked around. With the nearby trees for shelter and the wide open space around the lake, it would be easy to keep an eye out for potential threats, and plenty of places for the Ailura to rest for the night.

He nodded. "Looks good to me."

"Alright then. We should head back for the others." Sienna rolled to his feet.

"Already?" Indigo asked, raising his head.

Sienna shook himself off, but didn't seem any drier. "Well... yeah. Of course."

"Why?"

"What do you mean, 'why'? We have a job to do, and I'm going to do it."

"I'm sure they won't mind if we take a moment to catch our breath."

"We've had all evening catching our breaths. Now it's time to head back. The longer it takes us to find a new home, the more chance there is of something terrible happening on our way."

"I guess so."

Sienna began to walk back the way they'd come. Still dripping wet, Indigo noticed him shivering in the evening breeze. He didn't know why, but he felt a slight twinge of guilt for that. The Lutra moved a little closer until their sides brushed, hoping that the warmth of his hide would help him dry a little bit sooner.

"So... back on Veramilia, you never did anything like that? Ever?"

"Never. Not that I can remember, at least. Play was for cubs before they were old enough to work." Even thinking back, Sienna's tone grew sombre.

"That's horrible. I can't imagine growing up like that."

"Well, it was just... life. Do the Lutra play like that a lot?"

"Yes, of course! We play with our friends, and families, and to get to know strangers. Sometimes just on our own. Sometimes there are rules to win the games but sometimes there is no point at all. On the day of the Festival, sometimes the whole village will play!"

"The Festival?"

"The Festival of Love. The Lutra village has one every year!"

"What's the Festival of Love? Is it for couples?"

"Not just couples! It's where we celebrate our love for life and our families, and for what we are. Even the Riverfolk come. We put together festival chains to wear and the Queen makes a speech."

"How do you find the time?"

"Oh, we have plenty of time! Indigna takes care of us as much as we take care of each other. There's plenty of food to go around. Healers heal us if we are wounded, too. Maybe when you settle in, you'll have that sort of time as well."

"I sure hope so," Sienna said, and afterwards, fell silent.

Glancing his way, Indigo was suddenly hit with the realization that when their journey ended, he might never see Sienna again. That thought was curiously distressing. Now that they had played together, Indigo felt he was starting to glimpse something that the Ailura had long kept hidden away.

He realized that he would be deeply dissatisfied if the Ailura went back to being as miserable as they had been on Veramilia. What was the point of coming so far only for life to remain the same? If the Ailura hated living so much, it might have been better if they had just let the mountain wipe them out.

The thought surprised him so much that guilt immediately set in. He felt his gills prickle with embarrassment.

"Even if you don't get out much… you could at least make time for the Festival, right?" Indigo asked after a moment.

Amazement turned Sienna towards him. "You think the Queen would let me go?"

"Oh, yes, of course! If you're coming with me, there's no way he could refuse."

"Well, then, yes… I'd love to."

Indigo looked over at Sienna, and their eyes met for a moment in the golden glow of the sunset. And, for some reason, that look was enough to make his skin grow hot. Indigo looked away.

"I am the Princess, after all."

"Princess…? Oh, uh, I've been meaning to ask about that."

"Ask about what?"

"Shouldn't you be a Prince? Isn't princess… and queen, for that matter… well, aren't they for… you know…"

Indigo blinked.

"What?"

"You know, females?"

Indigo blinked again, slowly, as though this was a new concept to him. Then he shook his head.

"I'm perfectly happy with being a princess, and my father is perfectly happy with being a queen. If a future ruler wants to change it, then they can!"

"Could you have a female Queen, then?"

"Of course. Kings and Emperors are also not unheard of, of all kinds."

Sienna shook his head slightly, as though this was a foreign concept to him. "So if the Queen – Shimmer – took a mate, she'd be…"

An odd expression crossed Indigo's face.

"The Queen already has a partner."

Indigo thought back to Tide. He hadn't seen him since he'd left him behind that night. He hoped his father wasn't worrying about him too much. A lump rose in his throat.

"Ah, right. So what is the queen's mate?"

As he looked up, Indigo realized that Sienna was waiting for him to explain further.

"The Queen's mate is… another Queen. The Lutra can have two queens, just as we can have two fathers, or two mothers, or two neutral parents."

"Wait…! You mean to say that–?"

Indigo broke in. "Of course! A Lutra can be whatever they want to be, and love whoever they want. We are fluid and free, like water."

"That's…" he took a moment to process this information. "That's insane."

"Why?"

"Well, it's just…" Sienna trailed off. He took in a breath, as though he was about to speak again. But then he didn't. There was nothing he could say that felt right.

"So long as everyone is happy, that's all that's important," Indigo said.

"I suppose it is. Still…"

"It's different to the Ailura?"

"Yes," Sienna said. "For us… our lives are planned out at birth. Cubs inherit the duties of their parents and the roles they were born with. Then they grow up, and it's their duty to have cubs of their own. It's all traditional. It's just the way we are. It always has been."

Indigo shivered, as though in a cold breeze. "Well, maybe it's time to change."

"The old ways are what makes us Ailura. Even if we could, I don't think the elders would take kindly to the thought."

"If you say so."

Although Indigo didn't say anything, Ailura culture was beginning to sound grimmer by the day. He shuddered at the thought of having his life laid out for him at birth, having no say in who he was to become. Leading a life outside of his control.

The pair walked on in comfortable silence for a time.

The sun soon sank over the distant horizon and the Mothering Moon rose. Indigo was entranced by the way it reflected in Sienna's eyes.

The next day, Sienna and Indigo set out once more, leaving the lake behind. Sienna's fur had finally dried overnight and as Indigo bounded ahead of him, he followed with almost as much vigour and spring in his step.

The terrain had started to slope days ago, but now the incline grew far steeper, slowing their progress to a crawl. The ground became rocky, the soil and plants tinged a rusty red. The undergrowth became gradually sparser, trees fewer and farther between. Slabs of red rock showed though the soil.

As they climbed up the steep slope, Sienna looked back towards Indigo, and saw the Lutra watching him strangely.

"What is it?" he asked, as Indigo caught up.

"Your fur is blending in with the rock face!"

And as the Ailura turned to glance at his tail over his shoulder, he saw that it was true.

They continued to climb, pushing on up the mountain until they were both panting. Soon the path sloped less and became narrower; the ledges they scaled hugged the rock face. While Indigo clung to the rocks with rubbery paws, Sienna walked the ledges as though he'd climbed them all his life, his long tail acting as a perfect balance.

Whenever the terrain levelled out, the ruins of Sienna's ancestors hugged close into the stone.

Finally they came to a wide plateau. The summit of the Red Mountain loomed above them, and a cave mouth yawned from a sheer rock face.

Around them a few scattered ruins of the ancient Ailura still stood, sheltered by the steep slopes.

"I think we've found our next camp," Indigo gasped, as he pulled himself up onto the plateau behind Sienna.

Sienna peered into the mouth of the cave, disappearing into the heart of the mountain. He looked around, at the ruins and the peak of the mountain rising above them. The river rushed down the mountainside in a series of rapids beside the plateau, creating glistening rainbows in the air.

Finally he turned back the way they had come.

He could see the river weaving below them, winding on its way to the sea. The lake they had played in the day before sparkled beautifully a mile or two below them, whilst the tiny shapes of the Ailura wandered beside it, their coats standing out against the cool tones of the foothills. The rainforest, at first a mere scattering of trees, became a lush array of green, rippled by the winds sweeping over the island.

In the distance, the sea reflected the deepest blues of the sky. The lonely shadow of Veramilia just barely rose above the horizon.

Sienna finally nodded, briefly overwhelmed with emotion.

"Maybe even the last."

Chapter 6

The Truth

The Tribe's journey from the lake to the mountain plateau went as smoothly as Sienna could have hoped. All around bellies were full and moods bright as the trees became gradually scarcer further up the mountain.

Sienna and Indigo walked either side of Blaze, guiding her and speaking with her.

As the terrain began to slope upwards and slabs of red stone showed through the soil, Blaze began to sniff the air. Sienna noticed a glimmer in her eye, just as she picked up the pace.

"What is it?" he murmured to her, quiet enough that the other Ailura wouldn't hear.

Indigo glanced their way, curiosity tugging at his whiskers.

"There is iron in the rocks here," Blaze whispered back.

"How can you tell?"

"It's the colour of rust. If you focus really hard, you can even smell it where the rain fell. The earth here is nothing like it was on Veramilia."

Sienna lifted his nose, closed his eyes, and found that she was right.

"What does it mean?" Sienna asked.

"This must be it – the birthplace of our kind."

The thought filled Sienna's limbs with a renewed burst of energy.

Several hours later, the Tribe ascended the narrow path up the rock face.

In single file they kept moving, kept climbing, higher and higher up the mountain, until finally they reached the old plateau and stood at the mouth of the cave.

Sienna's sides heaved as he panted, Blaze settled down to catch her own breath nearby, and Indigo rushed to lap water from the nearby spring. Once Sienna had recovered, he helped drag Rusty up by the scruff of his neck. One by one, the Ailura filtered onto the plateau.

Soon it was bustling with furry bodies and striped tails, with all gazes turned towards the cave's wide mouth.

Chief Blaze gathered a small party of explorers together to delve deeper – to uncover the secrets of the mountain and see if it was fit to be their new home.

"I think it'll be fine!" Scorch said cheerfully, as they settled down for the night. "But… if there *are* monsters in there, we'll kick 'em right out!"

In response, Rusty grunted quietly. The half-tailed smith hobbled away to sleep, and wouldn't be there to help advise the explorers.

Sienna's belly fluttered with nervous excitement.

The next morning, Blaze rallied the few she had chosen to venture underground. She, Indigo, and of course Sienna were joined by the cheerful Scorch, and the burly Flint, just in case they *did* happen to run into any monsters.

The Chief led them down into the depths of the mountain. The distant murmur of voices on the surface soon faded, the only sounds the gentle clicking of their claws against stone and the quiet gasp of their breaths.

It didn't get any warmer as they descended deeper – but much to Sienna's surprise, it didn't get any colder either.

It did, however, get darker and darker until Sienna found it hard to see anything at all.

He heard Blaze swear quietly as she stubbed a foreclaw on something metal, a loud clang ringing out throughout the tunnel.

Each of the Ailura started in shock.

"We should turn back," Indigo whispered. His voice echoed back at them from somewhere further inside.

Sienna huffed faintly in agreement, glancing back and forth in the dark, and yet seeing nothing.

"We could bring back a flame to light the way," he suggested.

"Wait," Blaze said. "Just a little further. If there's metal here, then that means we're close."

Blaze was stubborn, but surely even she could see that this wasn't going to work...?

They needed to find their way back out, and even now Sienna wasn't certain he could.

But then... he saw it. The faint gleam of metal pipes further down the tunnel. As they moved on further, he could vaguely make out Indigo's white spots in the dark. Finally an archway loomed over them, a faint white light shining from within.

Sienna's heart hammered. They continued on, and his ears turned towards the sound of distant running water. The Ailura entered a wide room where pillars of sunlight shone through rectangular holes that presumably overlooked the mountain slopes. It took a moment before Sienna's eyes adjusted to the sudden brightness enough to see scattered stone buildings untouched by the ages. Perfectly round entryways and rough-hewn windows bored into hollow stone monuments, too dark to see into.

Pipes ran the length of the ancient city, and Sienna could hardly guess what they had been used for. Though it was still too dark to see them clearly, Sienna suspected that the metal baskets mounted on the walls had once been used to hold fire.

The bare wall beneath the windows was decorated with ancient pawprints in red-brown ink, or textured with patterns of clay. As they ventured further into the city, Sienna realized that they all wove together into a massive mural of long-gone chiefs.

The shapes of Ailura covered the walls, old and proud. Ancient jewels shimmering with rainbows had been set into the eyes of the most prominent figures. The rest stared into space, their eyes long-rusted droplets of cooled metal.

"I... I don't understand," Indigo said with wonder, as he looked into the ancients' bejewelled eyes. "These are pearls from the rainbow clam. They live only in the deepest parts of the sea."

"Are you sure?" Sienna asked.

Indigo rose up onto his haunches, holding his necklace up to the light with a delicate forepaw. Sienna watched as the central jewel glistened in a thousand colours. "Certain."

They continued on, following the cavern's path beneath the mountainside. As Sienna admired the sheer size of the mural, his paw collided with something in his path. He looked down to see a rib bone skittering across the floor.

His stomach heaving, Sienna turned his attention to the ground at his paws. He'd walked into a skeleton. Ancient bones cast sharp shadows across the stone.

His heart sank.

"Blaze...?" he called out. "You need to come look at this."

She approached. So did Scorch and Flint, the same expression on each of their faces.

Indigo placed himself by the skull, looking into its hollow eyes.

"Is that...?"

Sienna nodded.

Indigo took a step backwards, and Sienna heard a faint click. All three of them turned towards the Lutra to see that he had disturbed another pile of bones. Their breaths quickened, and Indigo's eyes flickered wildly. He darted back towards his companions and shrank down against the rock wall.

Now that he was looking, Sienna could see bones in every dark crevice, skeletons hunched everywhere they hadn't thought to check.

This ancient city had also been an ancient battleground.

"Come on. Let's keep looking. Maybe these are the only ones."

Sienna was hopeful, but inevitably, he was also wrong. The deeper the Ailura went, the more carnage they uncovered. Miniature caverns that used to be dens now lay empty, cold and bare.

Finally, Sienna pushed his way into what had once been a forge. Indigo filed in after him, closely followed by the others. A pillar of light shone through a skylight above them, lighting up the forge with a natural brilliance that left them blinking.

In the sunlight, mosses and grasses had grown over ancient tools and wall carvings, vines winding around a set of white-bleached bones. This one had a metal spike punched through its chest, standing upright even after all these years. As Sienna crept in closer, he realized that this skeleton was different. Its skull was small, its ribcage long, and legs short.

"Is that...?" Sienna slowly looked up towards Indigo.

"Yes," Indigo croaked. "Why...?"

"Our legends say that we were driven from our old home by monsters, but..." Sienna cleared his throat, shaking his head. "This means that... that..."

Indigo stared at him gravely.

"No. That's not possible. We wouldn't. The Lutra are... We're a peaceful race. We'd never..."

"But... you did," Scorch said, quietly.

"The Lutra are the monsters... the traitors... that drove us from our home."

It was soon decided that the Ailura couldn't stay in the old city. There was too much history there, and too many 'lingering flames'... whatever that was supposed to mean.

Whatever the case, the Ailura didn't think it proper to make a new home among the bones of their ancestors.

"What should we tell them?" Scorch asked.

"The truth, probably," Sienna said, numbly. "That these halls have been ruined by bloodshed, and our ancestors weren't even put to rest."

"Where else should we go?"

This time, it was Blaze who answered. "We should probably keep on climbing, see if there's a place for us on the other side of the mountain."

Throughout all this, Indigo remained silent. Although none of them had said anything to the effect, he suddenly didn't feel as welcome as he had a moment ago.

His thoughts went to Shard, back in the Village of the Lutra. Her words, her prejudice. Had she known...?

The thought ate away at him.

Some time later, they left the city. As Indigo trailed behind, he doubted that there was still a place in the group for him. He wished for a moment that he'd listened to the cranky old healer, because now he longed to return home to his fathers and to his kind. Perhaps he ought to let them finish their journey alone?

Indigo looked up, picking Sienna apart from the other three by the slight limp in his walk. He longed to speak, but what his travelling companion would hear, the other three would too.

So, Indigo remained silent as they emerged into daylight, fading into the background as the Chief made the announcement that the city was riddled with ghosts. Panic flooded through the ranks that all the ancient legends were true – although Indigo noted, with a slight twinge of gratitude, that Blaze had left out the part about the Lutra.

As she made the speech, Indigo made brief eye contact with the half-tailed blacksmith. The ice in his eyes was enough to send shivers down his spine.

Indigo looked away from him quickly, heart pounding, and reminded himself that there was no way he could possibly know. There was no way any of them could possibly know.

Still, he knew they'd find out eventually.

The sound of voices eventually died down as the day faded into evening. One by one, the Ailura curled up and went to sleep, preparing for yet another day of travelling. It was only then that Indigo picked over the sleeping bodies looking for Sienna. He couldn't find the Ailura anywhere, but it turned out to be because Sienna had been looking for him as well.

After exchanging a whispered greeting, Indigo and Sienna left the sleeping tribe, climbing further up the mountain path until they found a secluded outlook. Together they revelled in the silence and looked up at the stars.

Indigo didn't know how to break the quiet. He knew what he wanted to say, and what he wanted to do. He didn't mind leaving, but for some reason he felt that Sienna alone should know.

"I've been–" Indigo started.

"Did you–" Sienna began, at the exact same moment.

"Oh, I, er... I'm sorry," Indigo stammered.

"No, it's okay, you go first," Sienna said quickly.

"No, er... that's fine."

They fell into yet another long silence, each one of them avoiding the other's gaze.

Finally Sienna spoke. "Did you know?" he asked. In the darkness, Indigo couldn't read his expression.

"I don't think anyone knows." Indigo answered. "Except maybe the cranky old healer. But I..." He shook his head. "I'm not sure."

"What makes you think that?" Sienna asked.

"She's just been acting weird. From the beginning,

saying that we shouldn't rescue you, because you'd hate us. Perhaps this is why."

Sienna grunted quietly.

They said nothing for a time, watching rain clouds creep slowly across the moons.

Indigo hesitated, taking a breath before he spoke. "I was thinking... I might head back to the village. I want to talk to her about it."

Indigo looked up at the stars, purposely to avoid looking at his companion. Indigo had known him scarcely more than a week; why was this so hard?

"And just... leave us out here?"

Indigo's heart lurched. "Well... yeah. I've taught you all I know. You can make it from now on, right?"

Sienna was silent.

In the moment that Indigo glanced his way, he looked doubtful. "Besides..." Indigo added. "I don't want to be around the day that the Ailura discover the truth."

"The truth has nothing to do with you, Indigo," Sienna said. "The Ailura were driven from Indigna centuries ago. Anyone harbouring any meaningful hate towards the Lutra is long dead. Why should it affect us now?"

"Your legends call us monsters," Indigo reminded him. "Legends that scare you even now."

"That's true, but..." Sienna hesitated. "The Lutra are fluid, you said. Perhaps legends are as well. There were pearls in that old city, remember? Pearls that the Ailura could never hope to find."

"What are you saying?" Indigo asked.

"I think... there's more to this. The Ancients didn't always hate each other."

"I suppose, but..."

"At least come with us until the top of the mountain," Sienna said.

Indigo hesitated. Finally he turned to look into his companion's eyes, glowing like coals in the moonlight.

"Alright, then," he said. "I'll stick it out until we get to the top of the mountain."

The Tribe set off again as soon as the sun breached the horizon. Much to Sienna's frustration, it wasn't just the two of them this time, although he and Indigo were allowed to take the lead.

Sienna couldn't blame his kin for wanting to get away from their ancestors' fallen kingdom, now knowing what lay within. Most refused to stay, terrified of the possibility of lingering spirits. The battle uphill was difficult with an entire tribe, but the day passed quickly and night soon fell.

Their next camp was less than ideal. The river had become no more than the smallest trickle, and with no trees to offer shelter the slightest sprinkle of rain soaked them to the core.

Before he settled down for the night Sienna approached Rusty, curled up and shivering by himself.

The blacksmith looked up as he approached.

"Sienna," he greeted. "I haven't seen you so much. How've you been?"

"Fine, thank you."

"That all?" asked the blacksmith.

Sienna nodded.

"So, what brings you? If you're looking for some smithing, you're out of luck... but I'm sure you know that already."

"Actually, I wanted to talk about the fallen city."

"Hm?" Rusty's ears flicked towards him. "Ah, yes. What about it?"

"It's just... you've been acting oddly around Indigo since you met him. Like you... know something about him?"

Rusty opened his muzzle to speak, then closed it again. "What brings you to me *now*, lad?"

Sienna's breath caught in his throat.

"You saw something, didn't you?" Rusty guessed,

before Sienna could find the words. "Was it something to do with the Lutra?"

"Well... yes." Sienna shuffled, rearranging his tail around his forepaws. "So you *do* know."

"A thing or two, yes."

"What do you know?"

"Not a lot. The years have made the memories foggy. But from what I remember... they wanted to change us, but we refused to abandon our old ways. So they crushed us, drove us out, and, so it seems, forgot about us."

Sienna shivered. "How do you know?"

"A Lutra found its way to the island, once, when I was very young. She couldn't believe we were still alive."

"So she knew about us?"

Rusty nodded.

"Why didn't you tell us?"

"We had a... falling out. That's when she told me about the Lutra's dirty pawprints on our history. I don't know what *she* thought would happen, but we fought..."

Here, Rusty raised his half-tail.

"...And left each other a parting gift. After that, I never saw her again."

Sienna stared at the long-healed stump, aghast. "So she bit off your tail and then just... left you? What was she trying to do?"

"Same as always, she wanted us to change. No regard for our ways at all. I tell you, I'll have a bone to pick with her if I ever run into her. If she's even still alive." Rusty dropped his tail back down onto the stone, and rested his head on his paws. "Will that be all?"

"Yes... Thank you, Rusty."

"Burn Bright, youngun."

"Burn Bright."

The next morning the Tribe set out for the summit once more.

The terrain levelled out as they drew closer to the peak, the Ailura's anticipation mounting. They picked up the pace until their panting was all that could be heard.

As the sun passed its zenith and began to sink towards

the horizon, Sienna realized that Indigo had fallen behind. He turned back, allowing the rest of the Ailura to pass him by. The Lutra's sides heaved with laboured breaths, and he didn't notice that Sienna had stopped until he bumped into him.

"Are you okay?" Sienna asked.

"I'm fine," the Lutra insisted breathlessly, pushing past. "I'm just... not built for this."

Sienna noticed that he moved with the slightest limp, wincing as he put the weight on any of his four paws.

"We should stop for a while. We've never gone this far in a day before. Not without water."

"I'm fine," Indigo repeated. "Besides, we're almost at the top."

Sienna looked ahead, and saw that he was right. The Ailura frowned slightly. "We should reach it by nightfall."

Strangely, he didn't feel as elated as he thought he would. Sienna knew that this would be where he and Indigo parted ways. And then the Ailura would continue their journey alone.

With the distinctive prickle of being watched, Sienna turned towards Indigo. Their gazes met for a moment.

From that shared look he could tell the Lutra was thinking the same thing.

Finally, Indigo looked to the path ahead.

"You should join Chief Blaze. You deserve to be the first to see your new home."

Sienna followed his gaze, seeing the long line of golden, red and orange as they made their zigzagging way up ancient paths in the iron-red mountainside. Blaze's dark form proudly led the procession.

Sienna shook his head. "Not without you there to see it too."

Indigo let out a huff. Sienna let him gently lean against his hide as they continued the climb, higher and higher up the mountain until their breaths steamed in the air and Indigo shivered by his side. Finally, the narrow line of Ailura began to fan out, moving, gathering, whispering, looking out over the twilight sky. Almost at the back of the pack now, Sienna and Indigo finally crested the mountain. They pushed their way through to where Blaze stood.

She turned towards them as they approached to stand beside her and looked out over the horizon.

"I... I can't believe it," breathed Blaze.

"It's so..." As Sienna trailed off, Indigo finished for him.

"...Empty."

And it was.

The mountain fell away into a gentle slope before dropping into a sheer cliff face. The ocean foamed against the rocks far, far below.

And, when the sea receded after the crash of each wave, he could see rubble piled in the shallows and driftwood debris that had piled up over countless ages.

This side of the mountain bore nothing more than the twisted skeletons of long-dead trees clawing at the sky.

Stone ruins, from humble mounds to great pillars of stone, huddled precariously on the edge of the cliff.

Distant islands rose from the ocean in spikes, shattered remnants of something more.

Sienna's blood ran cold with familiarity.

"It's..." Blaze croaked. "It's like Veramilia all over again."

"I think..." Sienna whispered, a chill running down his spine. "I think we did this."

There wasn't much else that they could do. The Ailura stayed up at the summit for one more night, and then began the long journey back down the mountain. The overall mood was sombre, but Indigo offered as many words of solace as he could.

"We'll go back to the Lutra village," he said. "I'm sure

my father will know of somewhere else on the island you can stay."

Reluctantly, the Ailura agreed.

Step by step, they climbed back down the mountain.

Soon, they rejoined the faintest trickle of the mountain spring, where the tribe drank their fill. As soon as the stream was wide enough to enter, Indigo slid into the water and immersed himself fully, splashing Sienna and sliding down the rapids on his belly.

For the first time since they'd left the city, he made Sienna laugh.

Once they'd rested, the Tribe continued walking until they reached the cave mouth.

Few words were exchanged until Scorch stepped forwards, with Flint and a small party of others at his back. Exhaustion was etched in the lines on their faces, pale markings reddish with dust.

But as always, his eyes were bright.

"Blaze! Er... Miss Chief Blaze..." he corrected himself with a nervous cough. "...I've been speaking with a few of the Ailura and... we wanted to ask your permission to return to the ancient city. A large number of us wish to see the work of the Ancients in person, and to properly lay our ancestors to rest."

Blaze listened, her ears perked forward, slowly nodding.

Seeing this, Scorch glanced back towards the group as though looking for help.

A small, flame-coloured Ailura stepped from the party to stand beside Scorch, seemingly answering his silent plea. Her eyes blue, her ears small and fluffy, and her nose blunt, she was quite beautiful.

Sienna could see that her belly was round.

"...And there are some of us who can't possibly travel much further," she added, entwining her tail with Scorch's. "Elders, pups, and mothers, for one."

"...For the rest, it would simply be our honour to restore the city to its former glory," Scorch finished, with a final nod.

Blaze glanced sideways towards Sienna. Hesitation,

nervousness, excitement... he saw all three flashing through her eyes.

Then finally, she offered them a nod.

An excited murmur rippled through their ranks.

"Yes," she said. "Bring the city back to life, and restore it with the fire of a new age. As Chief, I... I need to report back to the Lutra, but I will return."

That night, the Ailura moved among themselves, touching noses, rubbing pelts, and saying their goodbyes.

As Sienna touched noses to Scorch and Flint, he mused that this was the first time a goodbye had not been filled with sorrow.

Later that night, Scorch and the other settlers broke away from the group and went to reclaim their home in the mountain.

There were a few who remained with Sienna and Blaze out on the plateau: the young and strong, those that dreamed of adventure, and a few who were terribly superstitious. It felt quite lonely sleeping under the stars.

Sienna was surprised to see that Rusty remained.

He approached the blacksmith as the rest settled down to sleep.

"Aren't you going with the others?" Sienna asked, once he was certain the half-tailed smith was awake.

"I don't feel like sleeping among the dead just yet," Rusty chuckled. "Besides, I have things I want to do first."

"What sort of things?"

"Adventuring. Frolicking. Sightseeing, if you can believe it."

"What sort of sightseeing?"

"Well... The Lutra, she... always used to tell me how beautiful their village was. I've always wondered if it were true. You've seen it, lad... Haven't you?"

Sienna nodded.

"Was it beautiful?"

"Yes, it was. Surrounded by rapids, with a waterfall in the centre. I thought... didn't you refuse to enter before?"

"I did."

"Well, what changed your mind?"

Rusty fell silent. "Well, it might be my last chance."

"But you... could have done that the first time."

Rusty turned his attention away from Sienna, gazing out over the rainforest.

"Maybe I could have. But back then I couldn't have told that old flame that she was right."

"The Lutra?"

Rusty nodded.

"She'd be old now. Very old. But... If she's still alive, she deserves to know. "

"What... was her name? Indigo might know her."

Rusty shook his head. "He might. But it's not his feud. If she had wanted anyone to know, the Lutra would still remember us."

"That's true."

Sienna did not press further. Soon he moved on, quietly stepping around the sleeping bodies to where Blaze sat quietly by herself.

Indigo slept nearby, soft snores fluttering his gills.

Lying on his back, with legs splayed towards the stars and a sliver of drool at the edge of his mouth, Sienna didn't think they needed to worry about waking him.

Sienna settled down beside Blaze.

She didn't glance his way, but the slight turning of her ears towards him said that she noticed.

"What are you thinking about?" Sienna asked.

"I'm worried," Blaze answered, softly.

"What about?"

"About the city. And the Ailura returning to the island. What if the same thing happens?"

"It won't," Sienna said, wishing he felt as certain as he sounded.

"How do you know?"

"Now that we know what happened to our ancestors, we can try to change. For real, this time. Because... we know what will happen if we don't."

"That's true. I just... can't believe it... what we've done. We were so blind."

Sienna stole a glance towards where Indigo slept. "It wasn't *us* that did the damage," he said. "Just like it wasn't Indigo who drove out our ancestors. *We* have no reason to feel guilty, but we do need to protect what remains."

Blaze followed his gaze. "And as the Chief, I'll need to be there to see it done."

"Exactly. But I'll try my best to help every step of the way."

Blaze's red eyes gleamed. "Thank you, Sienna."

Unsure of what else he could add, Sienna offered a small dip of his head. "We should get some rest," he said, nudging her in the shoulder.

She headbutted him right back.

"Yes… we have a long journey ahead. Burn Bright."

"Burn Bright."

The next morning Indigo, Sienna, Blaze, Rusty, and the rest of the Ailura set off on the next leg of their journey, making their way down the mountain and to the lake where he and Sienna had played.

As they passed it, Indigo couldn't help feeling a curious sense of nostalgia, as though weeks had passed since, and not mere days. As they left it behind, he found himself wishing that the two of them had been alone to play in its waters once more.

The sun soon reached its zenith, then began to sink towards the distant horizon.

As they settled down to rest, Indigo noticed there were some faces missing. A group of nineteen had stayed behind at the ancient city, leaving fourteen to make the solemn procession back to the Lutra village.

Yet now, tonight, there were eight.

Sienna, of course, worried and fretted until someone broke word that it was a young couple who had gone first, sneaking away into the woods to claim an untouched ruin as their own. Seemingly in response to their boldness, others had quickly followed, dispersing from the trail and disappearing into the woods.

The next morning, they kept on walking, following the ravine towards the river's mouth.

Three more quietly sneaked away into the lush rainforest. Soon after, a young adventurer announced to the Chief her intent to strike out alone.

As the river swelled to its widest point, only four remained to complete their last leg of the journey.

Indigo, Sienna, Blaze and the grumpy half-tailed smith.

Tomorrow, Indigo would return home to his kin. It was a soothing thought.

As the sun set, the Ailura curled up together around a mushroom's ivory trunk, its curtain of vines and lichens trapping their warmth and protecting them from prying eyes. Its great cap sheltered them from the rain. Indigo settled down a little distance away, choosing himself a comfortable spot in the undergrowth. He took comfort in the sensation of it furling around him until he knew he couldn't be seen. Comfortable, quiet, and alone, he closed his eyes and tried to sleep.

But for some reason, no matter how tightly he squeezed his eyes shut, sleep didn't come.

Whenever Indigo thought of parting ways with Sienna and returning to everyday life, something felt hollow. He realized that he was going to miss their walks and their little talks, and their one-sided games.

Every time he thought about the end, he couldn't help but deflate, as though goodbye had already been said.

The trek down the mountain had, for a few days, kept farewell at bay.

But now it was imminent.

Indigo remembered his offer to take Sienna to the yearly Festival of Love, and wondered if he had really, truly meant it when he said yes. If they settled on the mountain slope, perhaps, but if Sienna chose to live far away, it might not be an option.

Indigo tossed and turned until the ferns recoiled above him, and he finally pushed himself to his paws.

They couldn't part without taking one last walk together. And the presence of the other Ailura changed things between them; it couldn't be tomorrow. It had to be tonight, when they could be alone.

They needed the chance to talk.

With quiet rustles, Indigo pushed through the undergrowth, darting among tree roots until he found a trailing vine overflowing with bubbleberries.

He jumped, scrabbling at the bark until he managed to pull one down, and then carried it over to where Sienna slept, pushing his way through the organic curtain. The Ailuras' warmth, and their combined smoky scent, hit him all at once. He dropped his prize and gently nudged at Sienna's side.

Sienna grunted, stirred, and looked up.

Indigo rolled the bubbleberry into his field of view.

"Would you like to play with me?" he whispered. "One last time, before we get to the village."

Sienna paused, and for a second, Indigo's heart sank. But then the Ailura shifted, rolling over onto his paws. His fur was an endearing mess, sticking up where he had been lying on it.

"Let's go," he said softly.

Indigo's heart soared. He nodded, picked up the bubbleberry, and pushed back through the curtain as he led the way to the riverbank.

Quiet rustles followed him through the undergrowth as Sienna walked closely by his tail. Some time later, the ferns pulled away to show the open riverside. Sienna picked up speed until they were walking side by side.

Without stopping, Indigo dropped the fruit, rolling it along the ground with nudges of his forepaws before batting it over to Sienna.

Sienna nudged it back, and the game began.

Back and forth, back and forth, the berry bounced. And suddenly the game that Indigo had played a thousand times with his kin felt new.

Some time later, rather than tossing the fruit back to Sienna, he sent it bouncing ahead of them with a powerful flick of his tail.

Indigo stayed behind as the Ailura went to retrieve it, and then, when the moment was just right... nipped the end of Sienna's tail.

Indigo burst out laughing, and took off the other way. Sienna bounded after him, their game with the fruit forgotten.

Indigo led him into the forest on a wild chase through the undergrowth, flowing around trees and roots, while Sienna came crashing after him with all the grace and subtlety of a roaring wildfire.

Indigo dipped, dodged and leaped, his short legs blurring and his lungs heaving, Sienna always moments behind.

Indigo suspected that Sienna was letting him win the chase; the Ailura's strides were longer, and his legs infinitely more powerful.

Soon, the Lutra was panting, sides heaving. With a final rush of energy, he burst out into an open clearing and tumbled to a halt in a bed of soft flowering moss.

A cloud of insects, wings glistening with delicate rainbow shimmers, fluttered out from the undergrowth, fleeing the weight of Sienna's paws.

Indigo looked up towards his friend, and then at the world around them, full of plants and life.

The creatures of the night called out to one another in the distance, and Indigo's whiskers twitched to the scent of freshly-fallen rain.

Dewdrops sparkled around them like chains of diamonds.

A pair of plumaries danced around one another, glinting gold against the light of the moons. They danced, entwining under the deep blue sky.

Indigo's gaze ventured past them and trailed up towards the stars, the moons, and the silvery light shimmering on the leaves. Reflective flowers glowed neon where they trailed from the trunks of trees.

"Are you alright?" Sienna asked, gently nudging at Indigo's side.

He realized belatedly that he had yet to stand. And yet... he didn't feel like he wanted to.

"Yes... I– I'm just catching my breath," he said with a sigh. "You should, as well. It's the perfect place for it."

Indigo watched his friend slowly follow the flying creatures with his gaze. The Ailura unhurriedly settled down, swinging his banded tail over his forepaws.

His russet fur shifted gently in the slightest breeze, his white markings bright against the dark.

The world around them was beautiful, it was true, and yet he found his attention held by the shifting expressions on Sienna's face.

Wonder, happiness, peace – emotions so rare among the Ailura, yet so often taken for granted by the Lutra.

Sienna wasn't looking at Indigo, and yet somehow that made him all the more entrancing.

As though sensing his gaze, the Ailura looked down at Indigo, and suddenly the Lutra felt heat surging in his fur, embarrassment prickling at his whiskers... and yet, he couldn't look away.

He was once again hit with the realization that when the Ailura were gone, he would miss their company. From their strange, stoic nature to the comforting musk of burned wood that clung to their fur.

Or... perhaps more accurately, he would miss Sienna. When they were gone, Indigo didn't know if the Ailura would return to see them. Whether he'd return to the festival as he had said.

But his excitement had seemed so genuine.

The ache in Indigo's heart surprised him. Struck him. He'd never felt like this before. Never when leaving his village. Not even when saying goodbye to his fathers.

"It's... beautiful here," Sienna said, catching Indigo off guard.

"It is," Indigo agreed.

"I just hope it stays that way."

Indigo raised his head, looking at his friend curiously.

"What do you mean?"

"Well, you saw what happened... what we did. I just hope we can stop it from happening again."

"You will. And besides, there's no use worrying about it now. You have a new home, a new village, and a whole new island to explore! If I were you, I'd be jumping for joy."

"That's true. But... there's still the visit to the Lutra to worry about. The Queen deserves to know."

"Why worry? The Lutra will understand. Except perhaps old Shard. But she's more bark than bite."

"What if they don't?"

"Then we'll deal with it! But I assure you, the Lutra won't worry. We are fluid like water. We adapt."

Sienna grunted, but Indigo realized he didn't seem convinced. "You say that, but..."

He trailed off.

Indigo couldn't find any words to answer him.

After a few moments of nervous quiet, Indigo racked his brains for something else to say.

"...You know," he began, eventually. "It's strange. It feels like we've known each other forever, but it's barely been a cycle of the Mothering Moon."

"I know," Sienna said. "It's gonna be hard saying goodbye, tomorrow."

"I know. Do you... know what you'll be doing after we're done?"

Sienna shook his head. "I'll probably return to our village and help put the ancients to rest. And I... I want to light a funeral pyre for those lost back on Veramilia. For... my mother, mostly."

Indigo nodded. "Ahh. Caldera?"

Sienna nodded, his ears twitching. "You remembered?"

Indigo nodded. "Of course."

He thought back to the village, to where both of his fathers were waiting. His last encounters with both Shimmer and Tide had been bittersweet at best, but Indigo could hardly imagine losing either of them.

"Do you... have another parent?"

Sienna shook his head. "My mother was all I had. That happened a lot on Veramilia. I don't know what happened to my father, if I ever had one. He probably starved."

Indigo winced.

He struggled for a way to lighten the mood, his whiskers lowering slightly. But, as though sensing his struggles, Sienna spoke again.

"Did you mean it when you said you'd take me to the Lutra's festival?" he asked.

Indigo raised his head. "Yes, yes, of course. Why wouldn't I?"

"Well, it just… seems wrong for me to butt in. It's the Lutra's festival. It's a special time of year for them, and I'm afraid that I might not… well, you know. Be welcome."

"Are you kidding? The Festival of Love is a celebration of everything! It's our way of celebrating our love for life, and our home, and our health. It's our way of mourning those we've loved and lost and welcoming new faces into our families. It's our way of showing our love for our brothers and parents and friends, and our…"

Indigo trailed off. Suddenly the world around him faded away; the sounds, the sights, everything. All that remained was the Ailura, and himself, reflected in Sienna's eyes.

"…Our partners."

And suddenly he knew why parting hurt, why the world suddenly felt so new. Why the thought of being away tugged at his heartstrings.

After a pause, the words tumbled out unbidden.

"And… I… I care for you, Sienna. Of course you'd be welcome." Indigo rolled onto his paws, his heart pounding. It was as though he'd lost control of his tongue. And yet… somehow, that wasn't it. "Maybe even… you know… more than that. As more than just a friend."

Sienna's eyes widened.

"… Indigo, did you… do you…"

The Ailura opened and closed his mouth.

The silence was suddenly too much to bear.

"I... I don't–..."

Indigo's brain finished the sentence for him, and suddenly Indigo regretted everything.

"I... I don't know what to say..." Sienna finally finished.

"Why not?" Indigo's eyes prickled. His heart ached.

"...Because I..."

Of course, this was a stupid situation; they were different creatures, from two completely different worlds. There was no way that Sienna would–

"It's because I... I've never felt like this before," Sienna admitted. His ears went back, his expression changed. He looked away. "I... care for you as well. Maybe even... in the same way."

Indigo sucked in his breath. His stomach felt as though he'd eaten a village of moths. And yet he too was stumped.

Sienna glanced away. "Indigo, I... I think I might be in love with you."

"I..." Indigo laughed, a little bit manically. But his eyes were welling up. "I see what you mean, now. About... not knowing what to say."

Sienna avoided his gaze, fur slowly fluffing out from nose to tailtip. His ears shrank back against his head.

Indigo didn't think he'd ever seen an Ailura look so pathetic.

But that wasn't what was important right now.

"We have to tell my parents," Indigo said.

Sienna's eyes widened. "Tomorrow?"

"Yes, of course! When else?"

"Don't you think that this... seems a bit too soon? I mean, we... I don't even know what we're *doing* yet. What we *are*."

"Of course not. If we're in love then they need to know!"

"Hold on, hold on! Nobody said that– and, don't you think they'll be a little, you know, surprised?!"

"Well, yes, of course! But they're my parents... they'll be happy for us."

"Wait..." Sienna seemed quieter now. "Indigo, listen."

Come to think of it, his response hadn't been as enthusiastic as Indigo had hoped. "What is it?"

"I know that things probably work different for the Lutra, but... this is a lot. I need to think about things first before we talk about meeting your parents. Plus, your people might not... you know... *like* us, after tomorrow. And that's saying nothing of the Ailura."

Indigo felt frustration rising inside of him. "You don't know..."

He trailed off. Frustration rose in his belly, and he recognized it as the same sort of frustration that he felt when trying to convince Tide to go to the Festival each year. Quite suddenly, Indigo found himself thinking back to what Shimmer had said.

And suddenly, it clicked.

Shimmer wanted Tide to go to the festival as much as Indigo did; but what was more important was that Tide was happy there. If his father wanted to go to the festival, he would do it in his own time.

Bit by bit, Indigo's frustration crumbled.

"Alright," he said finally. "We can take as long as we need to."

Sienna relaxed.

They talked for a while longer, until the Mothering Moon began to sink in the sky. And then they returned to the mushroom where the others still slept, curled around its ivory trunk. Here they finally laid their heads down to rest; this time choosing to curl up together, in a tightly curled bundle of red and blue.

Chapter 7

Memories

The next morning, the party followed Indigo on the final leg of their journey in tense silence.

Although he didn't speak much as they walked, Sienna was torn, his emotions swinging between nervousness and disbelief. Occasionally, he'd steal a glance sideways towards Indigo, uncertain whether the events from the previous night had really happened, or whether he'd just had a strange, but beautiful, dream.

The look in Indigo's eyes suggested the former.

Either way, Sienna was certain that what he'd said was the truth. Even if it wasn't love, there was certainly something between them. Friendship, perhaps. Understanding.

Nevertheless, Indigo's presence made the world feel fresh, and brought a new life into his heart that he might not otherwise have known. Since his mother's passing, Indigo's playful nature and vibrant optimism had helped to fill the void she had left behind.

They came to the secret entrance of the village before Sienna was properly prepared for it. In daylight the entrance was an inconspicuous hole in the ground surrounded by roots and half-covered by ferns. They entered without much hesitation, and other than brief complaints from Rusty about the water washing around his paws in the tunnel, the remaining distance was cleared quickly and easily.

The stench of fish went from subtle, to difficult to ignore, and finally became overpowering enough that Sienna felt faintly sick.

Soon, they emerged from the dark and into the cavern filled with the roar of the waterfall. They blinked and took in the sight of the village.

Sienna heard Rusty draw in a sharp breath.

"Goodness me, she was right," he mumbled hoarsely, looking around. As Sienna turned to look at him, he saw a seldom-seen look of wonder on the blacksmith's face.

The waterfall spray glittered in a shaft of sunlight, rainbows arcing from the roaring pillar of water. The Lutra went about their daily activities, some carrying flowers and herbs, others carrying the catch of the day. Trading, talking, pups wrestling, their bodies moving and entwining in chaotic harmony.

Some watered or rearranged the flowers growing atop their dens, such gardeners hurrying to and from the stream with cheeks full of water. Occasionally they bumped into the fisherfolk transporting their catch by the rapids, the weight of the water carrying baskets up and down the slopes.

Almost immediately, the first of the Lutra noticed their presence. And as soon as one noticed, the word spread like wildfire, excited chatter filled the air and Lutra swarmed around them and their princess.

"You're back! What happened?"

"Did you find a home?"

"Obviously not, or they wouldn't be back here!"

"Are you sure? I was certain there would be more."

"Well, there's one more than last time, see?"

The three Ailura stood around awkwardly, flicking their tails. Rusty's ears lowered against his head, blocking out the din.

Indigo cleared his throat, rising up onto his haunches as he glanced around with as serious an expression as he could muster. Whilst a few looked at him expectantly, precious few of the voices actually died down.

"Excuse me? Excuse me!"

A few more voices quietened. Indigo could at least be heard over the clamour now.

"We must speak to Queen Shimmer. Alone."

It took a few moments for Indigo's request to be processed. And then the Lutra began to scatter, one by one. The crowd dwindled, gradually exposing a pale shape at the very back of the crowd.

Even as everyone else began to scatter, Shard remained. Her expression was sour, and her eyes narrowed, her scarred eye lending her a distinctly ominous bearing.

As soon as he caught sight of her, Sienna's fur began to prickle upright, a shiver running down his spine. But she wasn't looking at him.

"Shard...?" Rusty's voice brought Sienna sharply to attention.

"...Rusty? What are *you* doing here?"

"I'm just... I... It's been a while."

"Longer than that," Shard said. As though realizing that all eyes were on her, she turned her gaze on the other Ailura. "All of you, for that matter. If you think you can stay–...?"

"Excuse me, coming through!" Shimmer's voice broke through the hubbub, cutting Shard's sentence short. Soon he approached, led by a young Lutra. "Ah, welcome back, all of you!" He trailed off as he saw the expression on Shard's face. "What... What's going on here?"

After a long pause, Shard shook her head. "I'll leave this to you, my *Queen*," she hissed to Shimmer.

"Oh no, you won't. That's an order," Shimmer said.

Shard froze. "You can't order *me*. I'm your mother."

"Like it or not, I'm also your *Queen*, Shard. Not even you are above our laws, as few as they may be."

Shard bared her teeth, but did not continue to leave. Instead she stood where she had been preparing to, legs stiff and the tip of her tail twitching, her gaze fixed on Rusty.

"Do you think we should go somewhere more private?" Sienna asked, once it was apparent that she wasn't going to try again. Out here, he felt as though the wandering eyes of the Lutra were boring holes in his back.

"Ah, yes. Of course. Follow me."

They did so, winding in between the small, domed dens and following the rapids down to the foot of the village. Rusty fell back as they walked, trying his best to walk alongside Shard, only for her to fall further and further behind.

Finally, he gave up and continued walking just a little way behind them, alone.

"So," Shimmer said, once they'd pushed their way into an empty but not unpleasant den. "What brings you back to the village?"

Sienna cleared his throat, feeling his gut clench with sudden fear. "Well, we... found things on our journey. The ruins you mentioned, for one... along with other things that we thought the Lutra ought to know."

He gulped.

Shimmer nodded. "Go on..."

"Well, for starters, the ruins. You told us about them before, but... did you know they were built by the Ancient Ailura?"

The look of amazement passing over Shimmer's expression told Sienna that he had not. "Are you sure?" he asked. "How do you know?"

Sienna glanced up at Blaze, who stepped forward. With certainty, she spoke.

"These ruins have the same architecture as our homes on Veramilia. The same shape and style, even the same layout of what used to be villages. They all have forges, just like at home, and in some places you can even see the ancients' claw marks in the stone."

"Are you certain? It could just be pure–"

"It's not a coincidence," Shard broke in. "They're right."

"Shard?!" Shimmer stared at her, aghast.

"Yes, Shimmer. A *Queen* would know that the Ailura lived here on Indigna, once. A long time ago." She looked at Sienna. "Now… what else did you find?"

Sienna nodded.

"We discovered an ancient city full of the bones of our ancestors. We knew there must have been a battle there… and… our legends said that monsters drove us out of our last home. We didn't discover any monsters, but… we did find the bones of a Lutra."

Shimmer shifted uncomfortably.

"So what you're saying is…?"

Sienna nodded gravely.

Shimmer sat up, and then began to pace, muttering, whiskers flickering in frustration. "That's impossible, the Lutra wouldn't… we wouldn't do something like that. Would we?" Shimmer looked towards his son, as though the younger Lutra would have a different explanation.

"I'm sorry, Pa. I saw it too," Indigo said, looking away.

"I… I don't understand. How could we have forgotten? How didn't I know about this…? Any of us."

Shimmer looked towards Shard, but the old one stared off into space.

"It's because it was outlawed," she said.

"Outlawed?" echoed Indigo. "What do you mean, outlawed?"

"It's true. The story was the secret shame of the queens of old. We are a peaceful race, yet on that night our ancestors shed the mantle of peace and killed dozens, driving the survivors out to sea."

"But why?!" Shimmer's extravagant drapes chimed as he turned towards her. "Why would the Lutra do such a thing?"

Rusty stepped forward, his old voice cracking.

"It's because we wouldn't change our ways," he said. "Our traditions destroyed half the island. The other side of the mountain has sunk into the sea… just like Veramilia. The ancient Lutra drove us out because we were destroying their home. Only… we didn't believe that we were the cause, no matter how many times they told us."

Shard looked up sharply.

"At least... Not until we saw it for ourselves."

The white Lutra held his gaze. "So... you believe me now?"

Rusty nodded solemnly.

Shard looked from him to Sienna and Blaze. "All of you?"

"We all saw the scars," Sienna said.

Shard snorted. "...Not that it matters now."

Rusty looked away.

Shimmer's gaze fixed intently on Shard. "If it was outlawed, then... how do *you* know?"

"Because I was the one who made it so," Shard spoke through gritted teeth. "When it became apparent that nothing I could say would ever change their minds, I realized it was pointless for us to keep the story alive. In a few generations, the Ailura would end up killing themselves off anyway.

"So rather than scaring our pups with stories of what had once been, I knew we would be far happier if we simply forgot. With the Ailura gone for good, the Lutra would never have to resort to such bloodshed again. And so, I spoke to the Queen. Cascade agreed that parents should never teach such an awful thing to their pups, and so it drifted out of memory."

Rusty shifted his paws. "Are you... certain you did it for the pups, Shard?"

"You can clam up. You never even *told* your kind– the ones who needed to know!"

"I... I didn't know–..."

"You did know! Of *course* you knew! You listened to my stories until my tongue was numb and the sea was winter-cold. You knew exactly what your kind had caused! But you *chose* not to believe it, not to tell a soul. And look where it got you! A dead rock, a dying tribe and a mountain belching your beloved fire."

The half-tailed smith remained silent, quietly wincing.

"So tell me, Rusty – what made you come crawling back, after all these years? Are you here to beg for forgiveness?

Because I can assure you, I'm fresh out of that."

Rusty shook his head.

"All I want is the chance to tell you that you're right. About everything. About our traditions, our history, our future... Even your village. It really is as beautiful as you told me all those years ago."

Shard still glared at Rusty icily, but Sienna noticed her whiskers slightly relax. She blew out a sigh. "Fat lot of good that is to me now. You only left me one eye to see it with."

"True," Rusty said. "And I'm sorry."

"Sorry won't change the past, or put the island back together. But... I'm glad to finally hear it."

"Do you... want to try again? From the start?"

Shard's eyes narrowed as she seemed to consider. A few moments passed before she answered. "Perhaps."

Rusty relaxed, relief etched in his brows. "I never thought an old flame like you would be so hard to tame."

"Did the years teach you nothing at all? Silly old breaker."

Sienna thought he detected a touch of humour in the old Lutra's voice.

He finally turned to Shimmer. "Do you think we should tell the Lutra, then?"

Shimmer hesitated, and then nodded. "If we don't let our pups learn from our mistakes, then they may as well learn nothing at all."

And to Sienna's surprise, Shard didn't object.

Before making the announcement, Shimmer first went to discuss the matter with his mate. After a while he returned, and on the ledge beneath the waterfall, called a village meeting to discuss matters of utmost importance.

It was here he revoked the last law of Queen Cascade, Tide's late mother, revealing to the gathered Lutra the tragic secret of their kind. He offered them the opportunity to teach it to their pups, not as a bedtime story or a tale of glory, but as a cautionary tale. The elders took the news with mixed reactions, ranging from disbelief to accusations of the greatest disrespect towards their beloved last queen. From the rest, while there was a great deal of shock and confusion, the announcement went quite well.

Although Indigo didn't think it would make a difference, the Ailura decided to wait in the shadows, listening to Shimmer speak, keeping out of the way of the Lutra until the initial shock had passed. No one searched for them, and when they finally wandered out into the open, they were greeted without too much hostility.

The gathering soon began to scatter and the Lutra went back to their chores, discussing the odd turn of events with neighbours and friends, and marvelling that such a tragedy could be so easily forgotten. Soon after, Indigo went with the Ailura to find a place to sleep.

He noticed, though, that Blaze was behaving strangely. She kept glancing at Sienna as though she wished to say something. When they reached the empty den, Indigo excused himself, saying goodbye to Sienna with a subtle bump of their cheekbones.

As the princess of the Lutra, he had things to do in the meantime.

When Indigo was gone, Sienna turned towards Blaze.

"What's wrong?" he asked.

Despite her nervousness, she hesitated. "Sienna, I... I've been wanting to speak to you."

"What about?"

"It's just... I can't stay here," she explained softly. "I have to get back to the Tribe."

"Already? Are you sure?"

"Yes... Especially after what we've learned. I'll admit, I've... been afraid of leaving the Ailura by themselves after what we saw from the mountain."

Sienna's ears lowered. "So you really think that...?"

Blaze nodded. "Yes, I... It's just... the blacksmiths. So many of them rode the rafts to reach Indigna, and they'll be going back to what they know. And with so much metal on the mountain... Who can blame them?"

"What else can they do?"

"Well, here's the thing... I've been looking at the way the Lutra use water power. I was... thinking we could perhaps try to learn from them. Fire is destructive, and yet water is adaptable. Perhaps..." she paused. "Perhaps we could even learn to combine the two."

"What do you mean...?"

"Well, I won't know until I try. But if I do succeed, then... It could be the start of a new age for the Ailura."

"A new age?"

"Yes. An age where we can put the mountains back together and show our ancestors that traditions really can change for the better."

"With you as its chief, it's possible."

Blaze's eyes twinkled. "It could take years, but..."

"It'll be worth it."

"Yes."

Sienna fell into silence, looking at his friend. Their journey was over; and so much had changed. He could hardly believe that it was all about to end.

"...So... What about you? Are you coming?"

Sienna paused, shocked into silence. It was as though he'd never even considered the possibility. "I... er... uhm... well, I..."

"–You have things to do here? It's okay, I understand." Blaze grinned.

"You... you do?"

"Of course! I've seen the way you've started looking at the Princess."

Sienna's ears flushed, his fur prickling with embarrassment. He opened his mouth, then closed it again. After a while, all he could manage was "do you really think it could work?"

Blaze winked. "Well, you won't know if you don't try."

Sienna's skin flushed even hotter. "I suppose I won't."

"So yeah. I'll... see you soon, I suppose?"

Sienna nodded. "I... yes. I won't be long."

"Of course you won't." Blaze playfully batted his nose with a paw. "Now... go get him, wildfire."

Despite himself, Sienna felt his vision blur. "Thank you," he said. "For everything."

"You too. I... couldn't have done it without you. And not just because you're a scaredy spark who wouldn't be chief... though, that still applies."

Sienna chuckled. "I wasn't scared! You just deserved it more."

"Give yourself at least a little credit! I think you could pull off being a chief just fine. Although, I'll admit, not many would have given up that sort of seat in a hurry."

Sienna nodded. A moment later, a thought struck him. "Will you be taking Rusty?"

"If he wants to, then sure... but I don't think the journey back up the mountain will do him any good. If we're lucky, though... he might like it here. He's dreamed of seeing it for so many years, after all."

"I think Shard might have secretly been missing him, too."

"True." Blaze let out an amused snort. A moment later though, she shook her head. "Regardless... I should be going."

Blaze stepped towards him, gently touching her nose to his. Over the pungent smell of fish he detected the faintest whiff of smoke and metal.

He committed it to his memory.

"Burn Bright," Blaze whispered. And Sienna saw the glisten of tears in her orbs of red. "Brother."

His throat closed up.

"Burn Bright," Sienna choked out. "Sister."

Whilst he'd started off trying to put his efforts towards something useful, Indigo's attention span had quickly waned. He had, as a result, began to engage in a wild array of chasing games, and told anyone who would listen about his adventure up the mountain.

At this point, he supposed, he deserved it. He would have been quite surprised if his fathers were upset about him letting loose now, of all times.

Just as he began to tire of these games, Indigo received word that one of the Ailura was looking for him. When he finally found the Ailura in question, he wasn't surprised that it was Sienna. He was, however, quite surprised to see that Sienna was alone.

The Ailura approached, gently touching his nose to Indigo's.

"Sienna...?" Indigo asked curiously. "What's going on?"

"I... I've just been thinking. About what you said the other night."

Indigo's heart leapt, his stomach knotting. "Yes, yes? And?"

"I think I'd like to give this... us... a shot."

"Ah, that's wonderful!"

"But I... I want to know about how the Lutra do things, and maybe we should... er... you know... keep it on the down-low. Some of them might be a little... you know..."

"Confused? Yes, yes, I agree. But they'll understand. Love is love, after all. We can't help it."

"...Even still. Can we take our time?"

"Of course," Indigo said. "But if you meet my parents, they might be able to help with that."

Sienna paused, ears twitching. He looked down at his paws. Indigo could almost hear his brain working.

"If... we do go and meet the Queens, what will that

make us?" Sienna asked, eventually.

"What do you mean?"

"Well, I'm just... not sure I'm ready to commit to anything... you know... permanent."

"Well, it doesn't need to be. Not right now. Visiting them won't make us partners. We decide if and when that happens."

Sienna gave a slow nod.

"So...?" Indigo ventured.

"Let's...Let's do it," Sienna decided.

Before Sienna even had the chance to properly reconsider, or really come to terms with what he'd agreed to, an excited Indigo was springing away from him and bounding up towards the waterfall.

"Where are we going?" Sienna yelled after him, as they hurried around the back of the waterfall.

"Up to the Queens' Quarters!" Indigo called back. "That's where we all live!"

As they circled the plunge pool via a path hugging tight to the cavern wall, the path ended sharply, in a rocky ledge behind the waterfall. Beyond this, a bizarre sight came into view from behind the glittering cascade of water.

A contraption of moving platforms, rocks and vines slowly turning under the weight of the water, gradually rose and fell in an endless cycle.

"What is that...?" Sienna breathed, eyes wide as he watched it.

Indigo trotted up to the very brink of the ledge so that he was right next to the rising platforms. Turning back towards Sienna, he giggled. "It's a lift, of course!" he said, as though it were completely obvious.

"A what?"

"Watch this," Indigo said. He waited for a moment

until a platform was on his level, and then hopped from the stone onto the lift, which carried him up, up and up alongside the waterfall. "Careful! It's slippery!"

"Is there no other way?!" Sienna called up the waterfall.

"No!" hollered Indigo, his voice becoming fainter as the distance between them grew.

Sienna danced from paw to paw, hesitating, his fur prickling briefly with fear. He craned his head back, and watched as the Lutra hopped from the moving platform onto a rocky overhang high above him.

Briefly, he reconsidered his choices. Surely it would be easier to simply ask Indigo to bring his parents down to meet him instead?

But then, as Sienna watched, he saw the Lutra's blue muzzle pop out to look over the ledge above him, eyes bright with worry. He shook the tension out of his head, along his spine and through the banner of his tail.

I've faced worse. I've survived a landslide, swum in the sea, and escaped a mountain spitting fire! he told himself. *I can handle a moving platform.*

He took a deep breath, then stepped onto the platform. His heart and stomach briefly lurched as his paws slid on a thin film of algae. After regaining his footing he froze, heart pounding, claws driving into the platform beneath him. He waited seconds that felt like minutes, frantically searching the rock face until Indigo came into view. Then he lunged, hurtling off the platform and onto solid ground.

"Whoa! Glad you could finally make it." Indigo joked, as Sienna caught his breath. "See? It wasn't that bad."

"Is there really no other way up here?" panted Sienna, looking down over the edge of the ledge. His vision briefly swam at the thought of falling, only to be swallowed up by the waterfall pool.

"Of course not."

"What if it breaks?"

"We jump."

Sienna looked at Indigo incredulously.

"What? There's the waterfall pool directly below us."

"I can't swim," Sienna reminded him.

"Well, it won't break. Come on, we're not here to admire the genius of Lutra watertech."

Indigo beckoned him onward with a flick of his tail. Sienna looked up to see that the platform opened up into the mouth of a tunnel, decorated with pearls and colourful seashells.

Indigo soon disappeared inside.

Paws briefly slipping on rocks slick with algae, Sienna followed him inside.

No turning back now.

As they carried on further up the tunnel, Sienna's paws sank into a layer of soft moss covering the cave floor. Away from the roar of the waterfall, it was surprisingly cosy inside the cave. Innumerable rocky shelves had been decorated with shells and glittering treasures, and a curtain of trailing lichens hid the entrances to other, smaller grottos.

"Dad! Pa!" Indigo yelled. "Are you in there?!"

"Wait a minute–" Sienna began. "You have two f–?!"

Sienna broke off sharply as a head emerged from behind one of the curtains of lichens.

Immediately, Sienna's nerves deserted him.

"Q-Queen Shimmer," he stuttered out a greeting with a small bow of his head.

"Sienna…? What are you doing here?" Shimmer asked, mystified.

"Is dad there too?" Indigo asked excitedly.

"He is."

"Do you… think he'd be able to come out and meet Sienna?"

Shimmer hesitated.

"It's just… We wanted to talk to you about something."

Shimmer looked from Indigo to Sienna. "I'm sure he'll be okay with just the four of us. No more surprises, I hope?" He waited until Indigo shook his head. Then Shimmer slightly bowed. "I'll go and get him."

Before he left, though, he turned towards Sienna. "Please, though… try to keep your voice low. And try not to crowd him too much."

And then he was gone.

"Indigo...?" Sienna whispered, as soon as he was gone. "Are you... certain about this?"

"Of course," Indigo said. "My dad is... unique, but when you get to know him, I'm sure you'll love him."

The lichens parted once again, and Shimmer chimed out into the open. A dark blue Lutra followed, glancing quickly over Sienna, and then awkwardly avoided his gaze.

Sienna noticed Shimmer's tail slowly wind its way over Tide's. As he did so, Tide relaxed slightly.

"So you... must be Queen Tide."

"Yes, that's right. How did you know?"

"Indigo mentioned you."

"Ah. I see." Tide looked towards Indigo, a sparkle in his eyes.

"And... you must be Sienna, of the Ailura?"

Sienna nodded, just as surprised.

"So..." it was Shimmer who spoke, this time. "What brings you two here?"

Before Indigo could speak, panic rose in Sienna's belly, and he broke in. "Actually, I just... wanted to... meet you," he managed limply.

Sienna felt Indigo glance his way as though about to protest, then slump a little bit. Guilt gnawed at Sienna's belly. He didn't look at his Lutra companion for a little while longer.

"You... You did?!" Tide asked. "Wh... Why?"

"I... Actually..." Sienna paused for a moment to think, his heart pounding. He glanced towards Indigo, then spoke. "It's... just, amazing to me. The Ailura can't have two fathers. We have one of each or just one, and that's just the way it's always been."

Tide nodded, exchanging a glance with Shimmer.

This time, it was the shining Queen in his extravagant drapes who spoke. "Well... The Lutra are far more fluid than that. As I'm sure my son has told you already... there are Lutra with two mothers or two fathers, or two neutral parents. There are Lutra with three parents, or four, or five. Tell me… does it upset you?"

Sienna listened, his fluffy ears pricked. Although the mere thought of it boggled his mind, he shook his head. "No, of course not… but how… how could you possibly choose?"

Shimmer smiled slightly. "It's not about making a choice. Sometimes it's just about seeing who makes you happy."

Tide finished for him. "Even if they're not quite what you expected."

Shimmer nodded. "So long as a family is happy, then there are no limits to what it can look like."

"So… what if…" Sienna shuffled his paws. "What if a Lutra was to choose someone else? Someone other than a Lutra? Now that the Ailura have returned, it's… well… it's possible, isn't it?"

Shimmer and Tide exchanged a glance.

"Well then… it would be a surprise," Tide murmured. "But… the Lutra would adapt, I'm sure. We'd do our best to make them feel safe and at home."

Sienna glanced towards Indigo, but the Lutra was looking away.

"Did… did that help?" Tide asked.

"Yes… Yes. It's… it's amazing, the way things work here. Thank you."

"Was there anything else?" Shimmer asked.

Indigo twitched his head to one side, but Sienna answered before he could. "A-actually…" Sienna stuttered. "There was one last thing…"

Epilogue

The Festival

It had been almost a full year since she'd made the journey to the village of the Lutra, and this time, of all times, Blaze was late. *Damn.* The sun was already setting overhead, the sky faintly tinted with copper. With any luck, she might be able to reach the village before sundown.

The other Ailura, she knew, should already be there. But, as both chief and lead engineer for the next generation of tools and techniques, she was kept busy by her work. She was close, so close to her next breakthrough. She could feel it in the tips of her whiskers.

But she'd promised Sienna that she'd be there. It had been too long since she'd seen her brother. Too long since she'd seen anyone, really, even if the duties of being a chief were poorly suited to a life of solitude.

All things considered though, things were going well.

Blaze's paws carried her fast along the riverbank, sides heaving, while a copper chain jangled softly about her neck. Whilst the Ailura blacksmiths rarely forged from scratch these days, the pieces remaining from repurposed tools made a fine festival chain for the Chief.

Soon she pushed her way through the foliage and into the tunnel, pressing forward until the roar of the waterfall rose up around her and the burble of excited voices thrummed up through her pads.

The Lutra were already gathering together on the central plateau, a myriad of shapes draped in an array of colours and glittering trophies. And in between them, the fewer, yet stockier forms of the Ailura, dressed in their own styles of chains as best as they could craft. Blaze recognized the slate-grey form of Flint and the mottled pelt of Scorch with a small, orange cub clinging to his back. And above them all, atop the rocky ledge where the Queen should have sat, were the familiar shapes of an Ailura and a Lutra.

Sienna's chain was formed of seaweed coils and sported a variety of bright-coloured seashells in overlapping waves; it wound its way several times around his neck and added a splash of colour to his dark furred chest. Indigo's, on the other hand, was a cobbled mess of vines and haphazardly-arranged flowers.

Despite biting back a laugh at the sight, Blaze was pleased to see that he wore it proudly.

Bright coloured flowers glowed in every corner of her sight.

As Sienna caught sight of her, his eyes lit up, and he waved his tail her way.

She offered an encouraging nod.

Indigo cleared his throat. She watched him step forward to the very edge of the ledge, before calling out at the very top of his lungs.

"Lutra!"

Seemingly taking his cue, Sienna stepped forward as well. "...And Ailura," he added.

"To each and every one of you, welcome, welcome!"

A hubbub of cheers and chatter rose. Indigo waited for it to die down before continuing.

"Lutra, you might notice something different about today's celebration. And that's because today we are celebrating a union! Not of partners, but of tribes. It has been almost a year since we welcomed the Ailura onto our island, and… since then, so much has happened."

Indigo glanced sideways towards Sienna, who spoke next.

"We've grown, we've learned, and we've changed. With our pasts entwined, and our futures bright, we are no longer two separate clans, but one kingdom."

"And, from this day forward, we hope the Festival of Love will not only be shared in by the Lutra, but celebrated by all. And to all those present who don't know, we celebrate tonight the love of our home, and our island. We celebrate our love for living and life itself! We protect each other, we aid each other, and we keep each other safe. Why? Because that's what love is. Love is love, and love is fluid and adaptable like water."

Sienna's tail curled over Indigo's, and the two's sides pressed together.

"…And no matter its form, it keeps us strong."

"And now," Sienna declared. "Let the Festival of Love begin! May you all Burn Bright!"

With that, the crowd dispersed. Blaze pushed her way to the front, the crowd swelling around her. Everywhere she went she caught flickers of recognition on their faces. She waited patiently for Sienna to make his way down to meet her, and when he did, his face lit up.

"Blaze! I didn't think you were gonna make it!"

Blaze grinned back. "Wouldn't miss it for the world. But if I'd known you'd be speaking, I would have been a bit more punctual!"

She playfully swatted at his nose.

"I doubt that," Sienna chuckled, ducking her paw and landing a swipe of his own.

Taken by surprise, Blaze laughed.

Indigo landed beside his partner, nodding a greeting her way.

"Where is Queen Shimmer, anyway?" Blaze asked.

"My parents are celebrating the festival in their own way," he said, twisting around to face the back of the crowd.

Blaze followed his gaze, and there they stood; Queen Shimmer and Queen Tide, watching from beyond the rapids away from the noise.

"It's the first time he's been to the festival in years. I've never seen him so happy at one before."

The Queens' tails were entwined as they watched their son, full of pride.

"Anyway," Blaze smiled. "I'm glad to see that you two are getting along."

"When haven't we?" Indigo asked, glancing up at Sienna with warmth in his eyes.

"I don't know about you, but I can think of a few occasions," Sienna said, with a wry smile.

Indigo looked his way, seemingly dismayed, then grinned as he saw the look in Sienna's eye. A moment later, he smacked the Ailura on the shoulder with a small forepaw.

Sienna chuckled. "How's the chieftain lifestyle treating you, then?"

Blaze shrugged. "Well, we're making a lot of progress. For now, we've been working on new methods of extracting metal from the mountain without damaging it too much. I've begun to make some breakthroughs when it comes to incorporating steam into the ancients' technology, too. It's more efficient than fire alone."

"Oooh, steam?"

"Yes, of course! It seems like some of the ancients' tools were built to use steam originally. It's just a matter of figuring them out."

"That's amazing!"

She noticed that even as he spoke, the Lutra's gaze wandered out across the crowd. The festivalgoers were beginning to merge into large groups, preparing to begin their dance through the village.

"We should join the parade," Sienna suggested.

Indigo nodded eagerly, whiskers flaring.

"Let's do it."

All three of them bounded away and soon were lost in the crowds. They wandered past the Ailura, in their colours of crimson, flame and ochre. And Lutra, weaving and flowing around them in tones from emerald and cyan to the blue of the ocean and the rich purple of the twilight sky.

Soon the two tribes danced, each and every beating heart in the village forming their own tiny piece of a vibrant living rainbow.

The End

Acknowledgements

(Written in December 2019, to family and friends)

If you're reading this, then you've reached the end of *The Forge and The Flood*. Our wedding will have come and gone, and Chris and I will now be married men. However, before you return this book to the memory shelf, I have a few final things I would like to say to those who helped me to bring this story to life:

Firstly, I'd like to thank Taylor. They read and helped edit the entire book to a professional level, all whilst knee deep in National Novel Writing Month (ouch!). As one of our best men, they also helped us with various steps of wedding planning along with Chris #2.

Secondly, I'd like to thank Alice, who in addition to offering company during long, long days of writing, helped provide feedback on the world and characters, asking questions that I never thought to answer.

Thirdly, I'd like to thank my younger sister Abbie, for being so enthusiastic and devouring every word even in the first, messiest drafts.

I would also like to thank you, the reader, for joining me in these pages and sharing our special day.

…And finally, I'd like to thank Chris. This is a word to my wonderful husband, from yours. You've been with me through highs and lows, thick and thin, and stood by me when things got tough. There are no words to truly express how much that means.

Thank you too, for the idea for this book, which originated over 5 years ago as a passing conversation in a noodle bar that has since closed down.

If you've made it this far, I'm certain this afterword will bring a smile to your face. If not, I'm sure you'll make it eventually.

Whilst the journey of the Ailura is over, ours is only just beginning. Thank you for 6 wonderful years, and here's to many, many more!

Afterword

(As of November 2021)

As you may have guessed, there's something a little special about the book you are holding in your hands. *The Forge & the Flood* was originally written as a wedding gift for my husband. The Ailura and the Lutra were based on our two favourite animals, respectively. Their journey, based on the process of self-discovery and bringing our families together, albeit with a few less bumps along the way. It's a book I never expected to reach the shelves except for those of the 16 families who received it in paperback on our wedding day.

I have to say, it's a little bittersweet rereading the afterword knowing everything that has happened in the world since. It's been one heck of a first year of marriage, that's for sure!

But, as we approach our second wedding anniversary, and enter our eighth year together, it seems only fitting that we should start by sharing this story that has meant so much to us with the world.

So I'd like to offer a huge thank you to a few of the folks who have helped out along the way, starting with my publisher Elsewhen Press, who joined the scene only a few months after our wedding, mid-lockdown.

It's been truly wonderful working with them, first on my debut, *Riftmaster*, and now on this. I'm so unbelievably happy that they saw something special in this wee story about adorable aliens with very familiar problems.

As always, they've done an absolutely fantastic job, and I hope you think so too.

Secondly, I'd like to offer another big thank you to Chris, but I won't gush about him any more than I have already. All you need to know is that I get very, very fidgety when working in lockdown, and I wouldn't want to inflict that on my worst enemy.

I'd also like to reassure all of those interested that he did indeed finish this book on our honeymoon. And that he cried. A lot.

Finally, a massive thank you to you, the reader I never expected to see. I hope you had an absolutely incredible time reading this, and that it gave you a tiny fraction of the joy that inspired it.

I hope you have a great day, and to see you again next time!

Elsewhen Press
delivering outstanding new talents in speculative fiction

Visit the Elsewhen Press website at elsewhen.press for the latest information on all of our titles, authors and events; to read our blog; find out where to buy our books and ebooks; or to place an order.

Sign up for the Elsewhen Press InFlight Newsletter at elsewhen.press/newsletter

Riftmaster

Tales of a cosmic traveller

Miles Nelson

How do you hold on to hope when you're being repeatedly wrenched between worlds?

College student Bailey Jones is plucked from his world by a mysterious and unpredictable force known as the Rift, which appears to move people at random from one world to another. Stranded on an alien planet, he is relieved when he meets a fellow human, the self-styled Riftmaster, who is prepared to assist him. Although curious about his new companion's real identity, Bailey hopes that, with years of experience of the Rift, this cosmic traveller can help him find a way to return to Earth. But first, as the two of them are ripped without warning from one hostile planet to another, Bailey must rely on the Riftmaster to show him how to survive.

Riftmaster, an adventure, an exploration, is concerned with loss, and letting go, while still holding onto your humanity and identity, even when life seems hopeless.

ISBN: 9781911409915 (epub, kindle) / 9781911409816 (264pp paperback)

Visit bit.ly/Riftmaster

THOMAS SILENT

or

Why there are no more mermaids

BEN GRIBBIN

When widower Angelo found a small baby on the beach twelve years ago, he decided to bring him up as his own son. A sign around the baby's neck said 'THOMAS SILENT', so that was the name he was given. Apart from other people's curiosity about his name, Tom's life so far had been happy and uneventful. When he wasn't at school Tom would help Angelo run the café in his beachside shack. One sunday morning Tom was in the café on his own when a tall, thin, old man called Phillimore came in to escape from the rain. He showed Tom seven bright blue-green stones that he claimed came from a mermaid's necklace. When Tom held one of the stones he could almost feel the rise and fall of the ocean. Phillimore left and Tom thought no more about the stones or the strange old man until Angelo died and the café shack was closed.

Six months later when Tom visits the deserted shack, he finds an envelope from Angelo and discovers what else had been found with the baby on the beach. Tom's simple life suddenly becomes a mysterious adventure that starts with a magical night-time swim to the shore of a strange land. He meets Coralie, a girl hiding in the caves on the beach with Phillimore. The people of the land are held captive to the will of an evil tyrant whose power comes from more of the blue-green stones, which he has been hoarding in the city of Murmur. Tom realises that he, Thomas Silent, is the only one who can defeat the tyrant and save the people of Murmur. But first he must understand the power of the sea-stones and discover his true self.

This delightful tale of real mermaids and mermen will enthrall any teenager who knows that they are special and have a great destiny waiting for them. Those of us who have left teenage years behind will equally relate to Tom's personal journey. We have all looked out from a beach and wondered what is over the sea, but so very few of us find out like Tom.

ISBN: 9781908168931 (epub, kindle) / 9781908168832 (144pp paperback)

Visit bit.ly/ThomasSilent

Fantasy for fans of Celtic mythology from Peter R. Ellis

Peter R. Ellis' thrilling fantasy series, *Evil Above the Stars*, appeals to fantasy and science fiction readers of all ages, especially fans of JRR Tolkien and Stephen Donaldson. Were the ideas embodied in alchemy ever right? What realities were the basis of Celtic mythology? Visit bit.ly/EvilAbove

Volume 1: Seventh Child

September Weekes discovers a stone that takes her to *Gwlad*, where she is hailed as the one with the power to defend them against the evil known as the Malevolence. September meets the leader and bearers of metals linked to the seven 'planets' that give them special powers to resist the elemental manifestations of the Malevolence. She returns home, but a fortnight later, is drawn back to find that two years have passed and there have been more attacks. She must help defend *Gwlad* against the Malevolence.

ISBN: 9781908168702 (epub, kindle) / 9781908168603 (256pp paperback)

Volume 2: The Power of Seven

September with the Council of *Gwlad* must plan the defence of the Land. The time of the next Conjunction will soon be at hand. The planets, the Sun and the Moon will all be together in the sky. At that point the protection of the heavenly bodies will be at its weakest and *Gwlad* will be more dependent than ever on September. But now it seems that she must defeat Malice, the guiding force behind the Malevolence, if she is to save the Land and all its people. Will she be strong enough; and, if not, to whom can she turn for help?

ISBN: 9781908168719 (epub, kindle) / 9781908168610 (288pp paperback)

Volume 3: Unity of Seven

September is back home and it is still the night of her birthday, despite having spent over three months in *Gwlad* battling the Malevolence. Back to facing the bullies at school she worries about the people of *Gwlad*. She must discover a way to return to the universe of *Gwlad* and the answer seems to lie in her family history. The five *Cludydds* before September and her mother were her ancestors. The clues take her on a journey in time and space which reveals that while in great danger she is also the key to the survival of all the universes. September must overcome her own fears, accept an extraordinary future and, once again, face the evil above the stars.

ISBN: 9781908168917 (epub, kindle) / 9781908168818 (256pp paperback)

And now. September Weekes returns...

Cold Fire

September thought she was getting used to transporting, but this time it was different. As far as she could tell, her appearance hadn't changed, she was still even wearing her school uniform. But in a London of 1680, others saw her as a lady of considerable social standing. She had been brought here to stop something happening that would give the Malevolence an opportunity to enter the universe. But she didn't know what. Her first stop would be a tavern, to meet Robert Hooke, and then off to see Sir Robert Boyle demonstrate to the Royal Society the results of his investigations of the phosphorus and its cold fire.

ISBN: 9781911409168 (epub, kindle) / 9781911409069 (256pp paperback)

About Miles Nelson

Miles was born and raised in the distant north, in a quaint little city called Durham.

He studied video game design at Teesside University, graduating in 2018. Since then, he has taken a step back from coding to work on his writing career, and has since led several masterclasses with New Writing North.

He has been writing all his life, and although Riftmaster was technically his fourth novel, he likes to pretend the first three don't exist. Whilst he is primarily a sci-fi writer who loves long journeys, strange worlds and all things space and stars, he has also had brief flings with the genres of fantasy and horror.

He often writes stories highlighting the struggles faced by the LGBTQ+ community, and tries to include themes of empathy and inclusivity in all he does. Even then, though, Miles stands firm in the belief that this is not the defining element of his stories. And although he tries to represent his community as best he can, these themes are never the main focus; because he believes that (in most cases) a person shouldn't be defined by their deviation from standard norms.

Outside of scifi and fantasy, he has a deep-rooted fascination with natural history, and collects books told from unique perspectives (be they animal, alien, or mammoths from Mars). The older, the better; his oldest book is just about to turn 100!

He currently lives in Durham City with his husband, Chris, who so far seems unworried by Miles' rapidly growing collections.

Lightning Source UK Ltd.
Milton Keynes UK
UKHW012354230822
407651UK00002B/115

9 781915 304001